MW00903307

HAW   Pb   97-2225

Haworth-Attard, Barbara

Dark of the moon

DARK OF THE MOON

Barbara Haworth-Attard

Cover and interior illustrations by Dan Clark

ROUSSAN
PUBLISHERS INC.

Roussan Publishers Inc. acknowledges with appreciation the assistance of the Book Publishing Industry Development Program of Canadian Heritage and the Canada Council in the production of this book.

Legal deposit 2nd quarter 1995
National Library of Canada
Quebec National Library

Canadian Cataloguing in Publication Data

Haworth-Attard, Barbara, 1953-
Dark of the moon

(On time's wing)
ISBN 1-896184-04-9

I. Clark, Dan II. Title. III. Series.

PS8565.A86505 1995   JC813'.54   C95-900231-6
P R9199.3.H36605 1995

A short version of this story written by the author entitled
Star to Heaven appeared in two parts in the November and
December 1994 issues of CRICKET magazine.

Printed and bound in Canada

DEDICATION

For my mother, Gertrude Margaret Haworth, and in loving memory of my father, Lawrence Haworth.

CHAPTER 1

"Scritch. Scritch. Scritch." Meaghan rolled over onto her back and groaned. Every night for the past week a rasping, scraping sound had dragged her from sleep. She propped herself up on her elbows and squinted at the clock's glowing green digits–11:30. She had been asleep just over an hour. The scratching continued. It was really starting to get on her nerves.

Meaghan swept the cotton sheet from her legs and crossed to the window, bare feet slapping on the wooden bedroom floor. She parted the lace curtains and leaned out, holding her long brown hair in one fist to keep it from falling over her face.

A yellow sliver of moon balanced on the uppermost spire of a pine tree standing tall and black against the dark night sky. There were no streetlights here and the stars shone brilliant silver in their frozen silence. The air was still and heavy with the heated scent of the fading June day. Meaghan heard the scratching again and leaned further out the window.

"It's the witch, you know." The voice was low and close, whispering next to her ear. Meaghan started, jerking her head up and solidly banging it on the raised window frame. She whirled around, tears stinging her eyes as she rubbed the back of her head. Laura, Meaghan's new stepsister, stood behind her.

"Yes, the witch," she continued. "She's probably burying someone, or digging in the dirt for worms to use in a spell." Laura was watching Meaghan closely to see the effect of her words.

Meaghan stared at the other girl a moment, then pushed past her and crawled into bed. She wasn't about to give Laura the satisfaction of seeing her unnerved by a stupid scratching sound. She hadn't thought there was anything left to bother her at this point. She already put up with the unnatural silence, except for the constantly chirping crickets. How anyone could stand all this quiet was beyond her. The soothing purr of city traffic and an occasional wailing siren, they were her favourite lullaby, a guaranteed sleep inducer. And the bugs in this place, especially the spiders: huge, meaty monsters lurking in the corners of the porch.

Meaghan flopped over onto her side and faced the wall, continuing her silent listing of grievances. The dark—'they needed an orange streetlight to push the dark away. In the two years since Dad had died, the night corners of her bedroom had become shadowy and ominous. She had needed a light to keep the blackness at bay. Mom knew she was scared and had tried to talk to her about it, but Meaghan couldn't tell Mom about the black that hovered around the edges of her mind; black hearse, black clothes, black circles under Mom's eyes, black yawning hole swallowing Dad. Tell Mom and the black would get her, too.

It was so dark here that she spent more nights awake than asleep, fighting for her life. She was fourteen years old. She couldn't very well have a night light, because then Laura would know.

Laura. She was the worst. This recently acquired stepsister was moody and sulky. Wrapped in tight, sullen silences, Laura spoke only when asked a direct question and then replied with a flat, single word. "Be patient," Meaghan's mother had told her. "Laura's got her own problems to deal with. She'll come around in time."

Exactly how much time was Laura going to need? It had already been a month since Meaghan's mother had married Evan, and they had moved from their apartment into Evan's white farmhouse. Even now, Meaghan could feel the other girl's eyes boring through the gloom that separated their beds, drilling into Meaghan's back.

O O O O O

"Is it always this hot here?" Meaghan asked Greg. They waited at the end of the lane for the yellow school bus.

"It's probably hotter in the city," Greg said.

Meaghan knew he was right. She could remember some days when she sat in their air-conditioned apartment rather than brave the melting city streets. No air conditioning—she mentally added it to her list.

Greg was a new experience, too—a little brother. He was a ten-year-old jerk, but mostly she got along okay with him.

Laura stood off to one side peering in a hand mirror, carefully filling in her lips with bright red. Pale, blue eyes had been heavily outlined in black. If she's putting her makeup on out here, Meaghan thought happily, Mom must scare her a bit. In a perfect world Meaghan's mother would unexpectedly arrive at the end of the lane right about now and see Laura. Meaghan looked hopefully back the way they had come, but it wasn't a perfect world.

"You look like you've been sucking blood!" Greg yelled to Laura.

"Vampire bait," Meaghan whispered loudly to Greg. They both laughed but Laura ignored them.

Meaghan watched her snap the mirror shut and drop it in her bag. Then Laura pulled her T-shirt over her head and stuffed it in on top of the mirror. She bent over at the waist and fluffed her short, blonde hair with red-tipped fingers. Meaghan's eyes just about left their sockets on seeing the tight, cropped top Laura now wore. Six months ago she and Laura had looked pretty much the same, but Laura had since "blossomed" as Meaghan's mother had delicately put it. Got a hell of a bod was how Meaghan put it.

"What are you staring at?" Laura had straightened up.

"Nothing," Meaghan said. She looked down at her own T-shirt and blue-jean shorts. *I look like a stickman drawing. You're jealous! No way! Well, yes way. You have to admit it, you want that body instead of this skinny one. Life was unfair!* Meaghan wondered if she was weird or had a multiple personality or something. For as long as she could remember she had all these voices jabbering away inside her head. Probably Joan of Arc had had the same problem.

Greg was running about, arms flapping, dive-bombing an irritated Laura. What was he doing? Oh yeah—vampires. That reminded her of something she wanted to ask him.

"Greg, do you hear noises at night?" Meaghan asked.

"What kind of noises?" Greg's arms dropped to his side, and he stopped flying around Laura.

"Well, like, scratching or digging sounds."

"I told her it's the witch," Laura said. She moved closer to stand beside Meaghan.

"Miss Sarah's not a witch," Greg said. But Meaghan thought

10

he sounded a bit uncertain. "Miss Sarah's a really old lady who lives next to us. You can see her place through those trees."

Meaghan followed his pointing finger to where a patch of yellow showed through thick spruce branches. She waded into the grassy ditch for a closer look. Now she could see a tiny, yellow frame cottage, with a screened front porch. The house was set back from the road, sheltered by trees. It's safe there Meaghan thought suddenly, black couldn't survive in all that brightness. She stared at it a moment longer, then climbed quickly out of the gully. It was burning hot down there, and some weird insect was rubbing its legs together, croaking like mad.

"It's a cute place," Meaghan said.

"Cute!" Laura snorted. "More like haunted!"

"There are some people who think she's a witch," Greg said.

"Why do they think that?" Meaghan asked.

"Because she's strange—different," Laura butted in. "She called Mrs Crawford once and told her Mr. Crawford was in trouble. Mrs. Crawford found him pinned under the tractor just like Miss Sarah had said. Lots of weird things happen around her. I've heard that people have gone down that road and come back remembering nothing." Laura paused. "Others have never come back."

Meaghan rolled her eyes. "You don't really expect me to believe that, do you?"

"Well, you heard the digging noises yourself in the middle of the night. Can you explain it?"

Greg pointed down the road and grabbed his backpack.

"Bus!" he yelled.

Meaghan followed him up the narrow steps of the bus and

11

flopped into an empty seat near the front. Laura pushed past, going down the aisle to the back of the bus. She sat next to her friend, Jennifer, and turned around to talk to two boys in the seat behind. The boys were in grade twelve. The cuter one was named Brad, and it was general knowledge at school that he was Laura's boyfriend.

Meaghan knew that her mother wouldn't be too pleased to know that Laura had a boyfriend that old. But then, Laura had been careful that Meaghan's mother didn't know. Or maybe Mom couldn't do anything about it anyway. Laura wasn't her daughter. Only Meaghan had to do what Mom said. Not that Mom had to worry about boys all over Meaghan.

She sighed deeply and shifted her legs. The back of her thighs were sweating and sticking to the vinyl seat. Already the road passing beneath the bus tires shimmered wet with heat. By the end of the day it would be baking.

She thought back to what Laura had told her about Miss Sarah. Meaghan was glad the bus had interrupted that conversation. The only time Laura had spoken to her, all Meaghan had wanted her to do was shut up. Her imagination had been working overtime, churning out images of windy, leaf-filled nights, flickering fires, grotesque shadows, and newly dug graves. Well, there was nothing like the smell of egg salad sandwiches and old gym shoes on a hot bus to exorcise the demons.

Laughter exploded from the back of the bus, and Meaghan could hear Laura's shrill voice, then thought she caught her own name. Laura was probably telling them about her noises. Suddenly, Meaghan saw blackness from the corner of her eye. She turned her head quickly but couldn't catch it in full view. That had never happened before; not here, not in daylight. She was badly frightened. She reached into her backpack and pulled out a book, holding it in cold, sweating hands, but she didn't open it. *A plan, you need a plan of action. Something to keep you busy.*

Meaghan nodded her head in agreement, then looked furtively to each side of her to see if anyone had noticed. Apparently not, but it was a close call. That's all she needed–people thinking she was nuts.

She opened the book, flipping through the pages to her bookmark, and began to read. Everything was under control again. She had her plan of action. She was going to find out what caused the noises. She was going to do some investigating.

CHAPTER 2

Meaghan stepped off the school bus, glad to escape from that metal oven. It wasn't much better outside, but the open space at least gave the illusion of breathable air. Greg immediately ran up the lane toward the house, but Meaghan stood looking through the trees at the splash of yellow.

"Hey, Greg!" Meaghan yelled. "Tell my mom I'll be up soon. I'm going for a quick walk."

Greg turned and waved to show he had heard, then continued running.

"Going to see the witch?" Laura asked. "Don't let her put a spell on you." She was rubbing her mouth, leaving long, red streaks on a white tissue.

"Like that ugly hex she put on you? You got raccoon eyes, by the way," Meaghan said. She left Laura scrambling for a mirror in her backpack and started up the lane, soon coming to where it divided in two.

Meaghan stopped and peered down the narrow road that wandered through the trees. It was strange; she must have walked by this fork a hundred times, but never seemed to notice it or if she did, felt no desire to explore it—until now.

She shifted her school bag to her other hand. The afternoon sun was burning her back through her T-shirt and the shaded lane looked cool, but her feet seemed reluctant to move.

What are you scared of? Laura's witch talk? She's not scared, she's careful. Wimp!

That did it. Meaghan turned down the road. Anything to shut up those annoying voices in her head, and she stepped into green—the rich, deep green of grasses bending from the side of the road; the cool, leafy green of maples and oaks, limbs stretching high above her, softening the sun's harsh light into a pale, dreaming green.

Not many cars travel here, Meaghan thought as she stepped over a deep rut. The road gently dipped into a hollow. It was strange how this road went down, while their drive rose in a steep climb to Evan's farmhouse. Well, her house, too, she guessed, though she didn't think of it that way.

She thought of the towering, ancient pines that lined their gravelled drive; their skinny, prickly arms guarding dark secrets. These trees were different, friendly and peaceful, something that had been in short supply in Meaghan's life since Mom and Evan had married.

It was strange having a man around. After two years of soft female voices, Evan's big boom made her jump out of her skin. It must have been like that before, when Dad was alive, but Meaghan couldn't remember Dad as big and startling. Everything about Evan was large—his hands, his feet, his beard, his laugh, and his hugs. Those hugs—every time Evan wrapped his arms around her, Meaghan was terrified she'd be sucked into all that largeness.

She rounded a curve and there was the yellow cottage. Meaghan studied the single window, the blue door, and the screened porch. It wasn't very large; in fact, their old apartment seemed gigantic in comparison. Her ears rang with the buzzing of insects and shrieking of blue jays as they darted from tree to tree. And then silence. Not a sound from the trees, from the lane, from the house.

The road shifted beneath Meaghan and her head spun. She staggered to a tree and clung to it, her eyes locked on the cottage. Knock on the blue door and things would change forever. Walk away and everything would remain the same—the white farmhouse, the blackness, Laura and Meaghan—just the same. *It's the heat. Your imagination. What's that yellow stripe running down your back? Let's go home. Home. What's home?*

A streak of blue shot across the road and Meaghan shook her head. Definitely the heat she decided, then wondered why she felt so cold.

She pushed open the small iron gate and slowly walked up the short path to the screened porch. Puddles of colour—red, orange, pink, purple—dotted the yard. Meaghan smiled at the sudden fantasy of seeds and bulbs thrown helter-skelter and left to bloom joyfully where they landed.

She knocked at the blue door, then stepped back, heart thumping. No one came and Meaghan, feeling brave now, pressed her nose against the screen and peered into the porch. A spitting, orange ball of fur shot out from under a wicker rocking chair and launched itself at the screen and Meaghan's face.

She screamed and stumbled backwards, falling down the porch steps and landing hard on her backside. Stunned, she watched the hissing animal cling to the door, viciously shredding the screen with teeth and claws. It must be rabid! And it looked like it was going to burst through the netting at any moment.

Meaghan ran down the path and was reaching out her hand to push open the gate, when she heard it–her scratching sound. It was coming from behind the yellow cottage. She nervously looked over her shoulder, but the wild thing was gone from the door. Left for good or lying in wait for her. Meaghan heard the scratching sound again. No way was she going to pass up the opportunity to solve this mystery.

She cautiously went around the side of the house and stood, mouth gaping. A garden stretched from the road to the distant woods at the back and up to the side of the cottage. Evan had a small vegetable patch behind the shed, but nothing like this. This garden was huge! And in the middle of it a woman turned the black dirt with a hoe. The witch?

"Hello there." The woman straightened up and began to walk slowly toward Meaghan.

Meaghan watched the tall, gaunt figure stepping around clumps of dirt. She was dressed in a green cotton skirt and a bright pink blouse with a bow tied neatly at her neck. *Probably left her black cape in the house. She's just an old woman. Is that a hoe she's carrying or a broom? If her nose is covered in warts, run! Shut up, Meaghan silently yelled. Those voices were getting out of hand.*

As the woman came closer, Meaghan could see that her legs were covered in thick, brown stockings, feet pushed into dust-covered Reeboks. Springy, grey coils of hair had fought their way out from beneath a green patterned kerchief and lay damply on her forehead. The woman wiped her hand on her skirt, then held it out to Meaghan, giving her a wide smile, toothy and brilliantly white in the night-black face.

"You must be that new girl come to live at the Somter house. Meaghan, that right?"

Meaghan awkwardly took the work-rough hand, squeezed it briefly, and let go. She tried not to stare at the face inches from her own but found herself fascinated by the web of wrinkles spun from cheek to chin. She still hadn't said anything and the woman was looking at her expectantly.

Meaghan's words tumbled out, falling one on top of the other. "Um...I'm Meaghan Russell. My mother married Evan Somter, but I'm still Meaghan Russell. I mean, I kept my own name, Russell, though Mom uses both names now, Russell and Somter. She puts a hyphen between them, you know." *Brain, you on vacation or something? Voices where are you when I need you?*

"Well, I'm Sarah Johnston, though most folks just call me Miss Sarah. I'm pleased to meet you." Miss Sarah wheezed and laughed her words all at once. Her breath whistled noisily through parted lips.

Meaghan pointed at the garden. "Is this all yours?" she asked. "Do you have someone to help you? It looks like a lot of work."

"I just do it myself, go at it day and night to keep it up." Miss Sarah said. She looked over the straight rows and smiled. "But I don't mind. I do love my garden."

She turned to Meagan again. "So I hear you come from Toronto. I guess you feel pretty lost; away from the big city, I mean. Kind of unsettling for you getting used to a new family. And me keeping you up nights too," she added.

Meaghan stared at the brown eyes, alert and young in the lined face, but old with knowledge. They were laughing at her. She felt no hurt, only curiosity as to how Miss Sarah could possibly know Meaghan was lying awake at night listening to scratching sounds.

"Stands to reason I would," Miss Sarah said.

Meaghan was bewildered. She hadn't spoken aloud, had she?

"The nights have been real quiet lately and sound carries when the air's still. I've been putting my onions in. I scoop out the dirt with the hoe, drop the bulbs in, and cover them up. That's what you've been hearing. You see, onions grow better when planted in the dark of the moon."

Dark of the moon! Black mud, black smell, black fear. The earth tilted crazily. *Dark of the moon.* From far away Meaghan could hear Miss Sarah still speaking.

"Plant onions in the dark of the moon and the bulbs grow fat." Miss Sarah cupped her hand as if she held one of those fat bulbs right there in her palm. "Plant them by the light of the moon and the green tops grow big. Look nice, but that's all they're good for–just looks."

Meaghan struggled to focus on Miss Sarah. "How can the moon make a difference to vegetables?" she asked.

"I can't really say." Miss Sarah looked surprised at the question, as if it had never occurred to her to wonder why. "It's just the way my mama used to plant and she taught me. Her and the Farmer's Almanac. It tells me when and what to plant; when the moon will be dark or light."

Meaghan felt a bead of sweat tremble on her chin, then drop away. She looked out over Miss Sarah's garden, breathing in deep the smell of the warm soil.

Living in an apartment all her life, she had never thought about gardens before. Mom had put a couple of pots of red *Impatiens* on the balcony, but it wasn't quite the same. It would be kind of neat to plant a tiny seed in that dirt, watch it grow under her care. Meaghan felt better now and–she searched around to identify the strange emotion–happy. She hadn't been happy since they had moved to the country. Perhaps Miss Sarah was bewitching her.

Something orange shot through the garden toward them. The rabid animal! Meaghan quickly jumped back, but the animal stopped and gently wound its body about Miss Sarah's leg. It was a cat—a big cat!

"You've met Moses, have you?" Miss Sarah asked. She reached down and picked the cat up. It lay contentedly in the woman's arms.

"Yeah." Meaghan watched the cat closely. Was this blissed out animal the same crazed demon that had tried to rip apart a door to get to her? Did Miss Sarah have any inkling that her cat was Jekyll and Hyde?

"Your mama's wanting you now, Meaghan. You best be going. You come and visit me any time you like. I don't get much company," Miss Sarah said. Meaghan couldn't tell what Miss Sarah's eyes were saying this time. It didn't matter. She could tell Laura that she had met the witch and had come to no harm. "Tell Mr. Somter to plant his onions while the moon is dark."

"Does he have to actually plant them at night?" Meaghan asked.

"No! No! Child." Miss Sarah threw back her head and laughed, mouth stretched open, teeth lined up straight and gleaming white. "Dark of the moon is when it's a new moon. The light of the moon is a full moon. I've just been planting at night because it's cooler then; I want to get my onions in, but the days have been too hot for gardening."

Meaghan waved to Miss Sarah, then hurried along the lane grinning to herself. Mystery solved. They all thought Miss Sarah was digging at night because she was a witch. Here, all along, she was smarter than any of them. She did her gardening at night because it was cooler than during the day.

Meaghan ran around the back of the farmhouse and bounced into the kitchen. Her mother was cleaning potatoes at the sink. Meaghan watched the long, curling peels fall.

"Oh, Meaghan, there you are. I was just going to finish up here and come looking for you. Would you set the table for supper and ask Laura to come down and help, too?"

"Yeah, Miss Sarah told me. I'll be right down after I put these books away." Meaghan ran up the stairs two at a time. She landed on the top step and stopped. Mom had been standing at the sink and had not actually begun to look for her yet. In fact, now that she thought about it, she hadn't even heard Mom calling her to come in. Yet Miss Sarah had said Mom was wanting her, even before her mother knew she wanted her. *Witch! She's not a witch—she just knew it was getting close to suppertime. Your mom wants you, she had said, but Mom wasn't looking for you.*

Meaghan walked slowly into the bedroom and dropped the book bag on her desk. Laura was lying on her bed, turning the pages of a magazine.

"Mom wants us downstairs to help with supper," Meaghan said absently.

"Your mom," Laura said. "Not mine."

"Okay." Meaghan spoke with exaggerated patience. "*My* mom wants us downstairs to help with supper. Is that better?"

Laura didn't look up from the magazine. "I'll be down."

"Yeah, right." Meaghan crossed her eyes and screwed her nose up at the other girl, then stomped down the stairs. Sure Laura would come down—when the food was on the table and not a moment before.

CHAPTER 3

Meaghan plopped down on the top porch step. She stretched out one leg and studied it carefully. How could Mom say there was no need to shave yet. If the hair grew any longer she would be able to braid it. Laura shaved her legs; the fine hairs were often stuck around the water ring in the bathtub for Meaghan to clean. She tucked her legs up underneath her. They were too disgusting to look at.

It was late Saturday morning, the best day of the week as far as Meaghan was concerned. No rushing down the lane and no sweaty bus ride over teeth-banging country roads. It was a good thing school was out next week; Meaghan doubted she could survive much more of that mode of travel.

It was quiet, well, what city people called quiet—no yelling, mall music or car horns. Quiet for Meaghan was nobody bugging her. Laura had gone into town with Jennifer, and Mom was working at the bank until mid-afternoon. Greg had hung around Meaghan for a while, hopeful she would do something with him, but she was tired of being dragged into the woods. Finally, Evan had taken him mini-golfing. She had felt so happy to see everyone go, she wondered if she was becoming anti-social.

It was just that she couldn't get used to having people around all the time. It had been her and Mom for so long, it was hard to take three other people elbowing their way into her life.

Meaghan shifted restlessly and got to her feet. Now it was too quiet.

Brown dust puffed around her ankles as she walked down the drive. It had not rained for a month. The skin on her arms and legs was lightly browned—nicely basted she told herself. At the store in the nearby town...could you call one store, a small church with a large cemetery, a tearoom, and an antique shop a town? Anyway, she had seen the men in their pickup trucks and billed caps gather to talk, their faces long and gloomy. They would sigh and shake their heads, complaining about the odd weather and spring planting, as they predicted a poor harvest.

Meaghan followed the drive to the fork and went down the lane leading to the yellow cottage. Over the past few weeks, Miss Sarah and she had become good friends. Meaghan had even discovered a shortcut through the trees between the two houses, but she preferred to come by the laneway. Laura thought the friendship weird and commented frequently about witches and their familiars. Meaghan tried her best to ignore her. Miss Sarah might be an odd choice for a friend, but she liked the elderly woman; she enjoyed their talks about gardening, school, and how things were going up at the white farmhouse.

Mostly, Meaghan loved the tiny yellow cottage, the screened porch, the glasses of homemade lemonade—it felt so safe. Nothing could touch her there.

She pushed open the gate and knocked on the blue door. When no one answered, she went around the side of the cottage. In the garden, near the road, she could see a pink wrapped head bobbing up and down. Miss Sarah was working on her hands and knees.

Meaghan jumped across the straight rows to reach her. Through the dirt, she could see tiny eruptions of shiny green.

Their garden at home was doing the same thing. Evan had let her plant all sorts of different vegetables, and Meaghan had been surprised by the unexpected excitement and pride she had felt when the first leaf had shoved itself through the brown earth.

"Morning, Meaghan." Miss Sarah sat back on her heels, face stretching in her wide smile.

"Hi, Miss Sarah," Meaghan said. "Can I help you with anything?"

"Well, you could pull some weeds. The dandelions and radishes are having a real tussle. I'm on the side of the radishes, though I don't mind the dandelions all that much. Make real nice salad, dandelions."

"Dandelions in salad?" Meaghan was doubtful. "Aren't they poisonous or something?"

"No," Miss Sarah said. "You use the new leaves, the tender, small ones. After the dandelions have grown some, then they become bitter—kind of like people," she added. She held out a basket and Meaghan saw it was nearly full of narrow yellow-green leaves with ragged edges.

"There's an extra trowel by the next row and some gardening gloves." Miss Sarah watched as Meaghan stabbed at a root. "You should have a covering on your head, child. That sun is mighty hot. You'll have heatstroke in no time being bareheaded like that."

Miss Sarah pushed herself slowly to her feet. She stood a moment stretching her back and wheezing, then reached into the pocket of her skirt. She pulled out a bright purple kerchief.

"Let me wrap this around your head for you." She picked up Meaghan's hair and slipped the kerchief under it.

"You sure have pretty hair, real long. My sister used to have hair like this. My mother said it was just like my great grandma's hair. She was mixed blood, my great grandma, white and black." Miss Sarah knotted the ends of the kerchief across Meaghan's forehead. "There you go."

Meaghan smiled weakly and touched the turban tied around her head. *You look so stupid. If you take it off you'll hurt Miss Sarah's feelings. What if someone sees you looking like this! Someone like Laura! Miss Sarah is being kind. Wimp!*

Miss Sarah chuckled as she pulled on her cotton gloves and knelt again. Meaghan looked suspiciously at the old woman. Could Miss Sarah read minds? Meaghan wrestled the top off a dandelion.

There had been a mind reader at the National Exhibition in Toronto last year. Of all the people in the audience he had chosen her to stand up to read her mind. Meaghan had gotten out of that place real fast. She didn't want anyone messing around with her head; she didn't want anyone knowing something Meaghan didn't want to know herself. It was all a trick anyway.

Meaghan sat back on her heels and rested. They had worked for a long time, occasionally talking but mostly silent. It was peaceful here, far removed from school, home, and Laura. The sun was at its highest, lightening the sky above her to a washed-out blue, and it was hot. Meaghan had to admit that it had been a good idea to cover her head.

Her ears heard the sound long before her mind registered it; a car or truck was speeding along the road, its radio thumping a loud bass. Meaghan stood up and looked toward the road. She hadn't noticed how she and Miss Sarah had been moving closer to it as they worked along the rows.

A red pickup truck's tires were kicking up a dirt cloud as it sped toward them. It slowed down as it neared the garden. Meaghan saw three people sitting in the cab and two more in the back. A boy leaned over the low side of the truck.

"Black witch!" he yelled.

The truck was opposite them, then past.

"Nigger woman!" Laughter floated on the air to Meaghan. She couldn't move. She was frozen; frozen on this hot, hot day. It felt like her own tongue had formed and spat out those terrible words, but she knew it hadn't. She was going to throw up right here in the garden.

"Don't fret, child. I've heard worse than that." Miss Sarah gave a weed a final tug, then climbed to her feet and looked out over her garden.

"I'm glad to see hating isn't your nature. Isn't natural to Laura, either. She just hasn't learned that yet." Miss Sarah gathered her trowel and basket. "Noonday sun is too hot for working. Let's go up to the house and have some lemonade." But she didn't leave right away. She just stood there, her eyes following the straight, green rows. "I do love my garden," she said finally and walked toward the yellow cottage.

Meaghan stumbled after her, feeling her insides and outsides shaking. Miss Sarah had seen. Meaghan had desperately hoped she hadn't, but Miss Sarah had seen Laura sitting in the front of the red pickup beside Brad.

Miss Sarah went in to make lunch and Meaghan sat rigidly on the edge of a white wicker chair. She wanted to go home; be sick; scream at Laura; tell Mom; but she didn't know how to leave. Miss Sarah carried in a tray of chicken sandwiches, two glasses full of ice, and a pitcher of lemonade. Meaghan's stomach churned. She would never be able to force food down her throat ever again but automatically took the sandwich Miss Sarah held out to her.

"I'm sorry," Meaghan said softly.

"No need for you to be sorry. You weren't sitting in that truck." Miss Sarah patted Meaghan's hand.

"I know," Meaghan whispered. "But I just feel so bad."

"Eat your sandwich. It'll settle your stomach."

Meaghan took a small bite and chewed. *Miss Sarah's right; you didn't say those horrible things. Why do I feel so awful then? I never thought of Miss Sarah as black, she was just...Miss Sarah.* Meaghan swallowed and took another bite. *Miss Sarah was black, Meaghan was white, the sky was blue, and the grass was green. It was just colour, something you saw with your eyes, not your heart. How could people say such hateful things to each other.*

Meaghan crammed the last of her sandwich into her mouth and reached for another. Boy, she was angry. Angry that someone else's hate had rubbed off on her and she would never be rid of it again.

She watched Miss Sarah calmly rocking and sipping lemonade but noticed her sandwich sat untouched on the table beside her. Meaghan could feel rage rise red hot from her feet to her face. This was one thing Laura wasn't getting away with. Laura had hurt Miss Sarah. She hated Laura.

"Hatred's mighty powerful. It can sweep you up and carry you along before you know what's happening. You have to be always on your guard." Miss Sarah continued gently rocking. "My folk know hatred, all sides of it."

Meaghan thought about the kids in her class in Toronto. There had been lots of different nationalities, more than there were in school here, but she had never really thought much about it. They were just kids, like her. She knew about racism from teachers, television and radio news, but it was always somewhere else—somewhere far like South Africa, Los Angeles, Detroit. Never here; never touching Meaghan, until now.

"My great grandma came to Canada from South Carolina to escape hate. She was a slave on a cotton plantation. They worked her hard and mistreated her until she couldn't take it any more. She took my grandpa and ran away. She came to Canada on the Underground Railroad. Saved many a slave's life that railroad, including hers. Good thing, too, or I wouldn't be sitting on this here porch talking to you."

Meaghan gaped at Miss Sarah. Here was someone who was actually a piece of history. She must be over 100 years old, Meaghan thought. Miss Sarah crinkled her eyes, threw back her head and gave her wheezing laugh.

"You're thinking I'm old. Well, I'm eighty-three. You were thinking I was about 183." Miss Sarah was quiet a moment then spoke softly. "There were some mighty fine people helping runaway slaves get to Canada. You see, Meaghan, for every one person who hates, there's five who don't. They're the ones who give me hope; those five."

"You said your great-grandmother, but what about your great-grandfather. Didn't he escape with his wife?"

"Back then black folk couldn't marry. They were the property of white folk and property doesn't get married. My great-grandfather was sold away from his family and never seen again. Isn't that a sad story? But there were two sons. My grandpa had an older brother." Miss Sarah pushed herself up from the rocking chair. "I'll be back in a minute. I have something I want to show you."

Meaghan sat thinking. What would it be like to be owned, not be thought of as a person, just property—someone else's belongings like a shoe, a car, or a house? Miss Sarah came back to the porch carrying a small tin box.

"This here box came all the way from South Carolina with my great-grandmother." She held it out to Meaghan. Meaghan turned it over, scattering bright silver rays over the porch floor and wall. It was rectangular in shape, about the size of a book. Something clinked when she turned it over. Without thinking, Meaghan opened the lid and peered inside.

Her eyes were blinded by silver light. Meaghan jerked up her head, blinking to push the bright spots away, but the colours all around her melted and ran together, then faded to grey, then black. A loud noise, like rushing wind, filled her ears. Only the hard metal box, tightly gripped between her hands, was real.

She could hear the rise and fall of Miss Sarah's voice, so faint Meaghan had to strain to hear her.

"If you want to understand about hate and the reason why black folk fought so hard for freedom, you're going to have to know about everything—about picking cotton until you think your back's going to break, about fear so heavy in your belly you keep working and working. All your life hungry and tired. So very, very tired."

CHAPTER 4

Meaghan tugged another cotton ball from the bush with raw, torn fingers. She had been doing this for hours—long before the sun had shone pink over the horizon. Reach, pull, drop, body bent double; yet her bag never seemed to get much fuller. The air was heavy and thick, too solid to breathe. Meaghan could feel sweat, sticky and itchy, running down her sides. Her tongue was dry and swollen from thirst. Was there going to be no end to this heat wave?

A stab of pain shot up to her elbow. Meaghan yelped, jerked her hand back, and looked at the red drop of blood bubbling on her thumb where a twig had jabbed into it. Her eyes filled with tears as she shoved it in her mouth and sucked a moment. She caught a sudden movement out of the corner of her eye and quickly bent over.

Dust-covered brown boots, stitching coming loose at the seams, slowed, then stopped next to her. Meaghan's heart thundered in her ears—the overseer. In her mind's eye she could picture the black whip coiled loosely about his shoulder, never far from his reach. It was enough to pull her head back down and set her hands to scrambling. The brown boots didn't move and Meaghan began to tremble. Why didn't he go on, walk further down the row, watch someone else? Because she wasn't working fast enough, that was why. Her fingers were fumbling now, stiff and useless. She had never been so scared in her life. *Fear heavy in your belly....* She had heard that recently, but she couldn't remember where just now.

Another pair of boots, black and polished to a glossy sheen, joined the overseer's. These boots hadn't been in the fields much or seen hard work. It must be the master. Meaghan's hands shook so badly she dropped a piece of cotton into the dirt at the toe of one shiny, black boot.

"This one of the new ones?" drawled a voice.

"Yes, sir. Brought her from Virginia last night. She's young and she's strong so I put her in the field."

"Skin's so light you'd have to look twice to make sure she wasn't a white girl."

The overseer merely grunted.

"What's her name and what did you pay for her?" Meaghan heard the dry rustle of paper.

"Name's Meaghan. Price was 900 but I got her for 850," the overseer replied.

Eight fifty? Meaghan was completely bewildered. They'd paid money for her? What were they talking about? She was a person, a girl, you couldn't buy people. It must be a mistake. Should she tell them? But Meaghan knew it would be dangerous to even raise her head and look at the master, let alone tell him he was wrong.

"Seems healthy," said the master.

"Yep. Appears to be."

"Well, see she stays that way, she looks to be of child-bearing age real soon. I don't want you cutting her up with that whip of yours like the last one, you hear?"

"Yes, sir." Meaghan heard the resentment and fear in the overseer's voice.

The two pairs of boots moved further down the row and Meaghan went limp with relief. Then she felt a slow burn of anger colour her cheeks. They were talking about her like she was a prize breeding cow.

She thrust her hand out to the next bush, but stopped in mid-reach. Cotton! What was she doing picking cotton? Overseer! Master! How did she know who those people were?

She stood up and looked wildly about her. She was in the middle of a field of snow. Snow? When she was sweating like a pig? No, it looked more like someone had dumped a huge bag of cotton balls onto a field. Where was Miss Sarah's porch, the yellow frame cottage, the road? She touched the dress she was wearing. It was rough and scratchy, threads catching on the tears in her fingers. Where were her blue-jean shorts and T-shirt?

Panic flooded Meaghan's legs, urging her run. It didn't matter where, just fast and far.

"Girl, girl!" Meaghan whirled about at the hissing whisper.

"Get workin', girl. You ain't fixin' to run, are you? Not with Master in the field."

Meaghan peered through the bushes beside her and saw a black boy crouched, cradling a full sack of cotton between two large hands.

"Get fillin' that bag. We get them weighed every night and if you short, you get lashes." The boy thrust two handfuls of cotton to Meaghan under cover of the bushes. "Here, take some of mine. You'll soon get used to pickin', though you'll never be as fast as me." He grinned at Meaghan, mouth stretched wide showing white, big teeth. Meaghan had seen that smile before, but not on his face.

Meaghan took the cotton he gave her, stuffing it into her

sack. She began picking again. *I saw this breakdown coming. She was never very strong. There must be a logical explanation. A logical explanation! She's nuts that's what.* Great, it didn't matter where she went, it seemed the voices came, too. If they would shut up a moment, she would be able think this through.

She had been sitting on Miss Sarah's porch, and Miss Sarah had handed her a tin box. Next thing she knew, she was in a field picking cotton. The voices were right. She was nuts. She automatically filled her bag, not knowing what else to do. Her brain was too tired to think right now.

The sun was a large, red ball, sinking low through a grey haze, when a horn blew. *Red sky at night, sailor's delight.* There was no delight here. Meaghan raised dull, glazed eyes and saw the workers leaving the field. She had not known it possible for a body to be this exhausted and still be standing. Every muscle screeched with agony. She struggled with the heavy sack, trailing behind the others.

They were lining up in front of a shed. As each bag was put on a scale, a thin, short man with glasses recorded the weight in a book. The overseer stood nearby, whip looped over his wrist, as he supervised the weighing.

Meaghan joined the line. A black hand quickly shot back and shoved cotton into her sack. It was the boy who had picked opposite her. He didn't turn around or say anything, but kept his eyes intent on the ground. So Meaghan said nothing, either, not thank you or anything, but just stood there, dread knotting her stomach.

She wondered how he managed to pick extra. She was so tired, only fear kept her legs from buckling under her. She studied the boy's back as the line slowly inched forward. He was tall and skinny, his bony frame covered by a torn shirt and much mended pants. It was his turn now.

He bent over and as he hoisted his sack onto the scale, his shirt pulled up exposing his back. Meaghan gasped. Her breath sucked in with a loud, wooshing sound. Long, snake-like welts criss-crossed his back; some were old, white scars, others were newer, red and angry looking.

Rage brought Meaghan's head up, green eyes glaring into the small, pale blue eyes of the overseer. Two red, round spots stained the man's cheeks, but Meaghan didn't care. This man and his whip had done that horror to the boy's back.

She was at the weighing shed now. She grasped her unwieldy sack and managed to lift it onto the scales. Then she stood back. The overseer's face was twisted with fury as he roughly pushed aside the man marking down the weight to read the scale himself. It was eerily still. The overseer turned and shoved his face close to Meaghan's.

She saw thin, purple lips move in the black beard, white spittle foaming at the corners of his mouth, but she couldn't hear what he said. Then the face was gone. She felt a push from behind and staggered out of line. He'd let her go. She was okay. Her legs were rubbery and she doubted her heart would ever beat normally again.

"You shouldn't done that." A hand took her elbow and gently led her away from the weighing shed.

"Done what?" Meaghan was glad to see she could hear again. She was walking alongside the black boy who had shared his cotton.

"Be starin' at a white man. Especially when you got murder

in your eyes," the boy said. He gave a soft laugh. "Good thing Master wants you for makin' babies. You was pretty short of weight, and I could see from his eyes that man wanted to whip you bad."

They were walking on a packed, dirt path between a row of wooden huts. The air was heavy with a rancid stench that clung to Meaghan's clothes and skin. She retched far back in her throat, then tried breathing through her mouth. That helped a bit, but not much. Was there such a thing as a bath here, she wondered, or even a river she could jump into. She had never felt so dirty. She looked at the crudely built huts. There were no baths here.

"My name's Joshua." The boy smiled down at her. That smile again; if only she could remember...

"I'm Meaghan." She had to say something. Besides, talking made her feel almost normal, something she needed right about now. He had been kind to her and she wanted him to know she was grateful. "Thanks for your help back there."

Joshua waved her thanks away. "Meaghan," he said. "I never heard that name before. It's a pleasure to meet anyone who can stare Hendry down. Meaghan," he said her name again. "I like that name. You be sure you keep it. Keep your name and you'll always know who you are."

"What do you mean keep my name? Why wouldn't I? It's my name," Meaghan said.

"Some masters don't like your name, they change it. My daddy had one master in Alabama who named all his house slaves Sam. He said that way when he called he knew someone would always come running."

Joshua laughed, his head thrown back. Meaghan was horrified. How could he think that was funny? A name was so personal, yet could be changed on a whim, it seemed.

She looked up at him and couldn't help smiling. His laughter was infectious and erased some of the weariness from his face. Meaghan decided he was younger than she had first thought, only a year or two older than herself.

"Well, my name is Meaghan," she said. "And it's going to stay Meaghan."

"It's that kind of talk that earned me these stripes on my back," Joshua said. "Just try to keep that spirit mostly down inside. You can get in a heap of trouble showin' it around here."

Joshua stopped in front of a small, wooden hut. A tattered, red cloth hung over the door, a second one over an unevenly cut hole in the side.

"Come in, Meaghan." Joshua held aside the red cloth. "Come in and meet my mama."

It was dark inside and her eyes had to adjust to the dim light. She was standing in a tiny room, bare feet on a cool dirt floor. Where were her running shoes? Blue smoke hung from the ceiling and the mingled odors of grease, dirt and unwashed bodies caused her to swallow rapidly. She began to breathe through her mouth again.

Along one wall were two piles of rags with a single blanket spread on top. A small boy was sitting in the middle of it, solemnly sucking his thumb. These were their beds, Meaghan realized.

A woman, who had been crouched before a small fire, stood up as they came in.

"Mama, this here's Meaghan. She's just come," Joshua said.

He put an arm about his mother who smiled up at him. "And Meaghan, this here's my mama, Lanny."

The woman's head was wrapped in a kerchief—like Miss Sarah, Meaghan thought. Her skin reminded Meaghan of smooth, milk chocolate. She wasn't very tall, and the hand she held out to Meaghan was thin and frail. Soft, brown eyes studied Meaghan.

"How do you do," Meaghan said.

The small boy had slid off the pile of rags and buried his head in Lanny's skirt.

"And this is Daniel." Joshua laughed and swung the boy up into his arms.

"You'll stay and have something to eat?" Lanny asked Meaghan.

She didn't have anywhere else to go so Meaghan nodded her head. She was terrified, lost and alone, but she knew Joshua. Soon she would have to think about where she was, but for now her mind felt bruised and shattered, in need of rest. She would stay here, holding onto Joshua for her life.

Joshua dragged a wooden box to the center of the room. Lanny bent over the cooking fire and pulled the pot from the flames. She set the pot and three bowls in the middle of the box, then she, Daniel, and Joshua sat on the dirt floor. Meaghan copied them, glancing into the pot as she lowered herself. Her eyes widened in shock. It looked like water, with a few chunks of gristle and some wilted leaves floating in it. There was barely enough for one person to eat, let alone three work hungry people. Yet her body was so starved she greedily took the bowl Lanny handed her.

She looked around for spoons, but seeing none, raised the

bowl to her lips, sucking in a piece of the meat. It was tough and fatty, filling her mouth and making her gag. Lanny hurried to bring her a cup of water.

"Went down the wrong way," Meaghan gasped. She wiped tears from her eyes. She had managed to wash the gristle down with the water, but even thinking about it made her shudder. Then she noticed how quiet it had become.

Lanny, Daniel, and Joshua were sitting silently, heads bowed, hands joined around the box, while Joshua softly spoke a blessing. Meaghan stared at him. He was giving thanks—for this? That was it. She couldn't take another moment of this place. She wanted to go home. She began to cry noisily into her bowl.

CHAPTER 5

Lanny put an arm around Meaghan's shoulders. Meaghan sobbed hard for a few minutes, then took a deep, shuddering breath, but didn't move immediately from the comfortable circle of Lanny's arm. She picked up the hem of her skirt, dabbed at her nose, then reluctantly moved away from Lanny.

"I'm sorry," she apologized.

"Nothin' to be sorry about," Joshua said. "You're in a strange place with strange people. You're bound to feel all upset."

"I didn't mean to keep you from your supper. You go ahead and eat," Meaghan urged them.

Daniel was staring at her with wide eyes from across the box. Meaghan smiled at him, telling herself to be calm. She would never get anything figured out if her mind was in a constant turmoil.

She didn't want to face that watery stew again, but her stomach was growling. She carefully fished a piece of the leafy vegetable from her bowl and chewed slowly, staring at her bare feet, the floor, anywhere but at the floating chunks of fat.

Her eyes were scanning the side of the box when she noticed a patch of white against the brown wood. She reached down and her fingers felt paper. It was glued to the side of the box, but she managed to tear a small piece off.

The paper had yellowed and was thin, crumbling under her touch. She held it gingerly, close to her face to try to read it. A musty smell caused her nose to wrinkle. The paper was ripped through an ink sketch, but too little of the drawing was left for her to tell what it had been. The print was smudged, but she was able to make out four numbers, 1-8-4-7, in one corner, and farther down the page, the words "Elizabethtown, South Carolina."

"South Carolina!" Meaghan shrieked. "I'm in South Carolina?"

Joshua and Lanny exchanged a long look. "Yep. You must of come a long ways, if you don't know where you are. Nearest place is Elizabethtown," Joshua said. He was looking at her strangely, but Meaghan was beyond caring.

"And this 1-8-4-7, it's a date, isn't it? 1847!" She stared at the paper, unbelieving.

Lanny pulled Daniel closer to her, shrinking from Meaghan. Meaghan knew she sounded like she was out of her mind, but she couldn't help that. This was just too weird.

"That paper's old. Year's 1849," Joshua said.

Meaghan saw he was watching her warily. He was preparing to jump up and grab her if she went totally crazy and attacked them. *You're getting hysterical. Calm down. She just got hurled back in time more than one hundred years and you want calm! No one goes back in time; she's lost her mind. Well you just better look around and find it for her!*

Meaghan stared intently at the paper as if it might speak to her and explain how this had happened. People just didn't travel backwards in time, except on television or in books. Maybe she had fallen into a time warp or...she was asleep and dreaming. That was a good explanation; she could believe that. But then why could she smell, and feel, and eat. It was too real for a dream.

"You know what those letters say?" Joshua asked suddenly. "You can read?"

"Of course," Meaghan said. She spoke absently, turning the paper over and over in her hand, willing it to give up a clue. But the light in the hut was poor and the newsprint so faded she could only make out an occasional word.

"Where'd you learn readin'?" Joshua asked.

"At school."

The complete silence in the cabin eventually penetrated Meaghan's engrossment in the paper. She glanced up and found Lanny and Joshua staring at her, astonishment rounding their mouths.

"You went to school and you know how to read?" Lanny asked softly. She looked anxiously at the open door. "Can you write, too?" she whispered.

"Yes," Meaghan was surprised. "Can't you?"

The question was blurted out before she could stop it. She could kick herself. She had always taken it for granted that everyone knew how to read and write, and could still remember the shock she had felt when a teacher had told her that not everyone could read. Perhaps Joshua and Lanny were illiterate. Meaghan hoped she hadn't offended them.

"Blacks ain't allowed to read or write. White folks, they like to keep their slaves ignorant, not knowin' readin' and writin'. Guess they feel that way they'll always be smarter. Once someone can read and write, well, they might get pride and not want to be a slave no more," Joshua told her. "My daddy said that havin' knowledge was like comin' out of the darkness into the light. I expect freedom feels the same, like comin' out of the darkness into the light."

41

"Joshua! Be still. Don't talk that way. You don't know who listens." Lanny scurried to the door and peered out past the red cloth.

Joshua waved an impatient hand at his mother but lowered his voice.

"You better not let anyone know you bin to school and know readin' and writin'. Master particularly don't like his slaves knowin' much." He gazed admiringly at Meaghan and shook his head. "You can read and write," he repeated. He turned to Lanny. "That's what I want, Mama. I want to read and write; to know things. I want that for Daniel, too. I don't want him livin' like we do in a broken down hut, bein' someone's bought property, workin' hard for someone else every day of your life from the time you borned 'til you dead. It's what Daddy wanted for us, too." He leaned forward and put his hand over Lanny's. "I heard them singin' in the fields today, Mama, singin' 'bout heaven. Amos told me it's bein' fixed so some of us can run to Canada."

Meaghan's head jerked up. "To Canada?"

"I heard tell you just follow the North Star all the way. Amos said we can go, too, if we want, Mama."

"Joshua, please." Lanny pulled back her hand and Meaghan saw it twisting and turning with its mate in Lanny's lap. "Don't be talkin' 'bout such things." Lanny was looking fearfully at Meaghan.

Meaghan suddenly realized that Lanny thought she, Meaghan, was a spy. "You run, you just get caught, Joshua. Then they beat you until you crippled or dead."

"That's what master wants you to think, Mama. But lots get away, get their freedom. Canada's a big land. Master can't find you there and, even if he did, he can't touch you. There, a black person can walk right alongside a white person. That's freedom, Mama. Look at Daniel. He's gettin' older. I saw the traders lookin' him over. It's a good thing he's small for his age. They didn't take him this time, but it won't be long, after harvest maybe, and Master gonna sell him. I want more, Mama, for you and me and Daniel. If they catch me, whip me, it don't matter. I be dead already inside bein' someone's bought thing."

"Mistress won't let them sell Daniel. She knows I love that boy so much," Lanny said.

"She let them sell Daddy, and I know you begged her to let him stay. You work all day up in that big house, but Mistress don't see you. She don't see you any more than she sees the chair she sits in."

Meaghan had a vision of their closet at home with the vacuum cleaner, wet mop, and Lanny standing neat and tidy in a row.

Tears streamed down Lanny's face, though no sound came from between the tightly clenched lips. Meaghan wished Lanny would scream or yell her fear and pain, anything other than these silent, resigned tears.

She looked at Daniel who had crawled into Joshua's lap. He was so little. But he could still be taken from his mother and sold, and there was nothing Lanny could do but watch. Mind you, it also meant that she, Meaghan, could be sold.

Icy shivers ran up and down her spine. In fact, she had been sold. She couldn't come and go as she pleased. She was someone's property. She stared at Joshua. He was her only means of escape. He knew some people who were going to Canada. If she went, too, maybe she could find some way home.

Lanny stood up and shuffled between the fire and wooden

box. Meaghan went and sat at the door of the cabin, desperate for a breath of air. Others sat at the openings in their huts just as she did. Something wasn't right though, and it was making her feel twitchy and restless. Then she knew what it was. There were no voices, no one speaking. People were too beaten and tired to spare the energy needed to talk to each other.

Joshua came and sat cross-legged beside her. Meaghan looked at the weary slump of his shoulders, then shuddered at the memory of his back. He was tall, and with proper food filling out his frame, would probably be a fairly large man in her time. Back home he would be in high school, maybe playing football, no probably basketball—he was so tall—wolfing down hamburgers, being a kid. Living here, she looked back over her shoulder into the cabin, he had never been a kid.

"Will you write me my name?" Joshua asked. "I want to see what my name looks like in letters."

Meaghan picked up a small stick and drew a *J* in the dirt floor. "That's the first letter of your name," she told him. She added the *o s h u* and *a*.

"That my name?" Joshua asked.

Meaghan nodded her head. "Joshua." She said it slowly, pointing out each letter in turn.

"Looks like a mighty fine name, all writ out like that," Joshua said.

"Yes," Meaghan replied. She looked at Joshua. It was a fine name for a fine person. "Yes, it does," she repeated.

"Where do you come from?" Joshua's question caught Meaghan unexpectedly, and she had to scramble to find an acceptable answer.

"Up north." How on earth could she tell him where she really came from. *I'm from the future.*

"Virginia way?" Joshua was persistent.

"Uh...farther north than that." *So far you couldn't imagine.* Meaghan could feel tears stinging hot behind her eyes again. "I don't belong here. But I don't know how to get back home."

"Where's your mama and daddy?" Joshua asked.

"My mother's at home, but my dad...he died two years ago." Maybe she was dead. But wouldn't everything be black? That's what death was, wasn't it? Blackness.

"My daddy was sold when I was ten years old," Joshua said. He was tracing the letters of his name with a stick. "He never even saw Daniel. Daniel was borned about three weeks after Daddy left. We don't know where he is; Mama never heard from him again. He was a great man. When I was little I thought maybe he'd escaped, gone to Canada, and pretty soon he'd come take Mama and me and Daniel to Canada, too. Now I just think he's dead."

It was here; she could feel its black shadow creeping closer as Joshua talked. Even here the blackness came. She had to get home.

"Why do you call Canada heaven?" Meaghan asked.

"Cuz it's God's land. A land of milk and honey. Anywhere a man can be free must be heaven." Joshua's eyes were shining.

Meaghan thought about her time. Canada wasn't heaven. In fact, probably hadn't been even in his time. People didn't change that much. Hadn't she just heard those terrible things yelled at Miss Sarah? She opened her mouth to tell Joshua, then closed it. What was the point. He had so little, why destroy his dream.

Joshua reached out and lifted a few strands of Meaghan's hair. He held them loosely, letting them run through his fingers like brown water.

"Been wonderin' what this felt like all day long. Never been this close to such long hair." He let the last strands drop. "It feels pretty."

Meaghan could feel her cheeks burning. She'd never had a boy touch her hair before or say it was pretty. Her tongue was stuck to the roof of her mouth. Something else that didn't change with time travel, or in dreams, it seemed. She could never think of anything to say around boys.

Still, Joshua was amazing. Every morning he woke into this horrid ugliness, moved through it all day, and went to sleep knowing the next morning it would still be there. Yet he appreciated beauty...well, pretty.

"We best be gettin' in," Joshua said. He looked one more time at his name, then took his foot and rubbed the letters back into dirt.

$$\circ \quad \circ \quad \circ \quad \circ \quad \circ$$

The hut was dark and full of the night sounds of fluttering wings, insect clicks and chirps, and the occasional distant cry of something larger. Meaghan huddled miserably on top of a hodgepodge of rags spread over the dirt floor. Joshua had been angry to know Hendry hadn't assigned Meaghan a place to sleep yet, but Meaghan didn't care. She was desperate to stay near Joshua, even after she had seen the fear darkening Lanny's brown eyes every time she looked at Meaghan. Meaghan was different and that scared Lanny.

She and Joshua had a fiercely whispered argument in the corner of the cabin, while Meaghan sat trying to talk to a silent Daniel. If Lanny made her go, Meaghan vowed she would stay right outside the door. She wasn't leaving Joshua. He was her only anchor at the moment; her only means of finding a way home. The argument ended with Joshua dividing the rags and Lanny walking around stiff and silent.

Meaghan tossed restlessly, feeling the ground pressing hard against her hip. Her body screamed for sleep, but her eyes stared wide into the dark. Lanny had pushed aside the covering over the window, but between the cooking fire and the heat of the day it was unbearably hot in the hut. Meaghan was dying for a bath, some soap, her toothbrush, toothpaste and, after a disgusting trip to the ditch out back of the hut, a flush toilet.

Meaghan's mind reeled at the conditions Lanny and Joshua lived in and took for granted as they had never known any other. Yet, Meaghan believed that while Lanny was resigned to this life, Joshua was not. He knew there was a better life out there and he had the strength and courage to find it. Would that courage and strength have survived in her world? Or was it rooted here, to this time and place. Would he still pick up her hair and tell her it was pretty? Would he do that in her world?

That thought brought Meaghan back to reality with a cold, hard thump. How was she going to get back to her own time? First, she needed to know how she had gotten here. Had she been sucked into a time warp? Was she hypnotized or dreaming? Or had she fallen into a witch's spell—Miss Sarah's? The old woman's smiling face floated in front of Meaghan's eyes.

Meaghan sat straight up. Why had she not seen it before? It was plain as the nose on her face. Joshua's smile was Miss Sarah's smile. Or rather, Miss Sarah smiled exactly like Joshua. No wonder Joshua seemed familiar.

Meaghan lay back down on the rags. That meant that Miss Sarah was definitely the key to Meaghan being in this cabin, though it still did not explain how. This was useless. She was getting nowhere.

A cloth moved slightly against her foot, then Meaghan felt a stealthy skittering near her ankle. She lay stiff with terror, imagining rats, mice, and giant spiders. If anything ran over her she knew she would never stop screaming. Her fingers closed on a hard, round smoothness in the dirt beside her—a stone. She threw it to the edge of the rags near her feet, expecting an animal squeal, but instead there was a metal clink.

She looked quickly to make sure the others were sleeping, then crawled to the bottom of her bed. She searched around and found the stone she had thrown and continued feeling around until her hand scraped over a sharp object half buried in the ground. She hesitated briefly wondering if she was prying into something private, then began to clear dirt from around the object. She needed to know everything about where she was. She freed it from the ground and lifted it up. Moonlight from the window let her see what she held in her hand.

A tin box—it was a duplicate of the one Miss Sarah had handed to her that morning. Or, Meaghan thought, could it be the very same box passed from family member to family member until finally reaching Miss Sarah?

Something rattled inside. The lid was stuck from the damp, but Meaghan forced it open. She tipped it to one side, so the moonlight would fall into the box, then she leaned forward.

CHAPTER 6

Her body was trembling. Meaghan tried to open her eyes, but someone had glued the lids together. Finally she managed to pull them open. She was so tired.

"That gardening wore you out. You were dozing for a while." Miss Sarah's hand was on Meaghan's arm, gently shaking her awake.

Meaghan blinked and stretched, trying to force her brain to think.

"How long was I asleep?" she asked. Her tongue felt thick, and the words came out fuzzy.

"Not long, about half an hour," Miss Sarah told her.

"I had the strangest dream," Meaghan said slowly. Where was that awful stink coming from? It seemed to be—she lowered her head and sniffed—it was her!

"Did you?" asked Miss Sarah. She rocked contentedly, the chair moving back and forth on its bent runners, but she said nothing further.

If anyone told me they had a strange dream, Meaghan thought, I would want to know all about it; but not Miss Sarah. Meaghan looked blearily at the elderly woman, shrugged and yawned hugely. Gee, she was tired. She also felt sad, depressed. It was that same numb feeling she had had after Dad had died. What was the matter with her?

"I better get home. Mom will be back from work soon."

Meaghan stood up and took a step. Her legs were killing her. They were so stiff they felt like they were made of wood.

"Thanks for the lemonade, Miss Sarah. See you later," she mumbled and wandered down the lane. Her mind moved sluggishly, and she couldn't shake the feeling of gloom. Meaghan suddenly remembered Laura, the red pickup, the awful words. No wonder she felt so down. It was all Laura's fault.

The house was silent and Meaghan looked at the kitchen clock. It felt later but it was only a little after one o'clock. No one would be back for a while. She felt as if she had lived a whole day already. Maybe it was one o'clock tomorrow.

She yawned again and climbed the stairs to the bedroom she shared with Laura. It was hot and airless. Meaghan crossed to the window and raised it as high as it would go. All the heat in the house must float up the stairs and gather above her bed, Meaghan thought.

She stripped off her T-shirt and shorts and flung them onto Laura's bed, then flopped on her own bed and groaned. She felt like she had just run a marathon. She grabbed her pillow but snatched her hand back as pain shot up her arm. How did her fingers get in such a mess? They were red and scratched; the nails broken. Must have been the gardening.

She lay down again, carefully placing her hands on the sheet, sighed and felt herself drift. Through fuzzy, grey sleep she saw her hands as they had been that morning, covered by Miss Sarah's gardening gloves.

She was suffocating. Her legs and arms flailed wildly, while her lungs struggled to find air. Something was stuffed in her mouth.

"This is your stuff. Keep it on your side."

The muffled words woke Meaghan up. She grabbed her T-shirt from her face, tasting a salty sweatiness on her tongue.

"What's the matter with you?" Meaghan shouted.

"Your stuff was on my bed. This room is divided in two, see. All you have to do is imagine there is a line right down the middle." Laura was pointing to the floor and Meaghan followed the other girl's finger as it travelled up the wall. "That is your side," Laura continued. "And this is mine. Got it?"

Laura lay on her stomach on her bed and opened a magazine. Meaghan sat up and waited for the sleep to clear from her head. She was still tired. Maybe she was coming down with the flu or something. She didn't even have the strength to argue with Laura. Then she remembered.

"I saw you in that truck. You told Mom you and Jennifer were going to the mall," Meaghan said.

"I didn't lie, we did go to the mall. I never said how we were going to get there or when we were going, or even how long I was staying," Laura said. She flipped a page over, not looking at Meaghan.

"You knew Mom thought Jennifer's mother was driving you," Meaghan pointed out.

"Did you actually hear me say Jennifer's mother was driving us?"

"No, but that's what you let Mom think."

"What she thinks is her problem, not mine."

Meaghan was silent a minute, then she spoke in a low voice. "How could you yell such things at Miss Sarah?"

"I didn't say anything."

Meaghan jumped up and stood over Laura's bed. She glared down at the other girl. "You could have stopped them."

"Get on your own side of the room," Laura said. She pointed at the floor.

Meaghan sat back on her bed. Laura flipped on to her side to face Meaghan and began to laugh. "You looked so ridiculous in that purple turban."

Meaghan winced. She might have known Laura wouldn't let that go unnoticed.

"It was hard to tell which of you was Miss Sarah. You are so dumb."

"Those were awful things those kids said. They were worse than swearing." Meaghan was yelling now. She wanted to hit Laura, make her hurt.

"Grow up! She's an old lady. She probably can't even hear very well." Laura was getting impatient.

"She heard all right. You are such a jerk, Laura." Meaghan strode angrily to her dresser, yanked open a drawer and pawed through her clothes looking for clean shorts and a shirt. "No wonder your mother left and doesn't want you with her. Who would want someone like you?"

Meaghan could almost see her words fall, solid, slamming hard, and spreading hurt. *It doesn't matter. Laura's tough, she doesn't care about anything or anybody. Yes, she does. She cares as much as you. Good for you, that was telling her. Mom told you about Laura and her mother because she thought you would understand. She trusted you not to say anything. Give her a taste of her own medicine. You hurt her badly.*

Meaghan turned around from the dresser. Laura's face was white; even her lips were drained of colour. Meaghan saw the pain deep in Laura's eyes. She felt sick. Now she was the one hurting people. Look what being around Laura did to her.

Meaghan slammed the drawer shut, clutched her T-shirt and shorts to her chest and walked to the door. *Why am I wasting my time feeling sorry for her. This is Laura!*

"By the way, the door is on *my* side of the room. Guess you will have to climb out *your* window to get downstairs." Meaghan ran from the room just ahead of the flying magazine.

What a ghastly meal, Meaghan thought as she speared a tomato and examined it closely. Dream images of green leaves and gristle floating in greasy broth made Meaghan feel queasy, and she let the tomato drop from her fork.

"Not hungry?" Evan asked.

"I don't know. Not really I guess," Meaghan said.

"It's pretty hot. I didn't even feel like cooking anything for supper," Evan said cheerfully, but he looked from Meaghan to Laura.

"I'm glad you and Evan planted that garden, Meaghan. It's wonderful to have our own fresh salad fixings," her mother said. She smiled at Evan. "Meaghan and I are more used to the produce aisle at Loblaw's. Now we're spoiled, aren't we, honey."

Meaghan smiled wanly.

"You seem kind of limp tonight. I hope you didn't get too much sun helping Miss Sarah." Her mother leaned over and brushed Meaghan's hair back and felt her forehead. "No fever."

"Miss Sarah made me cover my head, " Meaghan told her.

Laura snorted. "Yeah, you should have seen her. She had on a purple turban."

Meaghan glared across the table. "Mom, can I be excused?" Her mother sighed and nodded.

Meaghan pushed open the screen door leading to the porch.

She started to plop down in a lawn chair when she abruptly jumped back up. She had forgotten to do her spider check. Sure enough, there was a web stretched across the two arms and a gross, fat spider smugly swinging in the middle. Meaghan shuddered. Gee, she hated them, and this porch, this house, and Laura.

She wandered down to the garden and walked listlessly between the rows. She bent down, momentarily distracted by a new green shoot coming up. She walked to the end of the row and looked at the stake she had hammered there. "Peas." Her mother came out of the house, walked over to Meaghan, and stood looking at the straight, green rows.

"Now what's this?" she asked.

"Peas," Meaghan said.

Her mother walked down the row a little, then turned back. "What's the matter?" she asked.

Meaghan hesitated, then decided she had nothing to lose. "Mom, this isn't working out. Laura hates me, I hate her. I want my own room. There's nowhere I can go that's my very own anymore." Meaghan kicked a lump of dry dirt with the toe of her running shoe. "I wish we had stayed in Toronto."

"I sometimes wish we had too."

Meaghan turned and looked at her mother. "You do?"

"At times," her mother said. She smiled at Meaghan's surprise. "Everything is so different here from the city. And different from when it was just you and me. I have three more people to think about, worry over, but when things get really bad, I think of Evan. He was the best thing to happen to me in a long time. He's a good man, Meaghan. And, of course, you. I count a lot on your support."

"I like Evan. And Greg's okay, but Laura..." Meaghan hesitated. *You're squealing—only rats squeal. You've always told Mom everything. It'll make you feel better. Squeak! Squeak!*

"Something happened today, Mom. I was helping Miss Sarah in her garden, then this red pickup came roaring down the road. There were kids in the back and they called Miss Sarah awful names. One in particular was horrible; in fact, I think it's worse than the f... word."

She remembered the icy coldness those words had sent through her veins. She kicked again at the dirt. *White cotton falling into the dirt by a black shiny boot.* Meaghan dragged her mind back to what she was saying.

"Mom." Her voice sounded like she stood apart from herself. "Laura was in that truck." Now that she had told her mother, tiredness washed over her again. She tried to make sense of what her mother was saying, but Joshua's and Miss Sarah's faces kept floating in front of her.

"People can be very cruel, Meaghan. I'm sorry it upset you so much, yet I'm glad that it did. I'm glad you have a big heart and you care about people."

Meaghan squirmed uncomfortably, remembering her hurting words and Laura's white face. Should she tell Mom about that? Maybe not. Squealing on Laura was one thing, squealing on herself, well, that was something altogether different.

Her mother was still speaking. "I thought if I gave Laura time she would come around. I know she's really hurting, but she doesn't seem to want to talk about it. I don't think there's anything worse than feeling someone doesn't want you. Maybe I went at this the wrong way."

Meaghan didn't answer. Mom sounded like she was talking

to herself anyway. Her mother put an arm around her shoulders and they walked back to the house.

"Honey, you look awful. I think you must have had too much sun today. Go to bed early and try not to worry. I'll have a talk with Evan and we'll see what we can do."

"I'm just going to stay out here a bit longer, okay Mom? It's too hot in the house. When you talk to Evan be sure to say the word air-conditioning a lot. Maybe he'll take the hint."

Her mother laughed and went into the house.

Meaghan lay on the hammock and pushed herself back and forth with the tip of one shoe, thinking about what her mother had said about Laura hurting. Greg and Laura's mother had remarried last year and had a new baby. Meaghan gathered that the woman had never been what you'd call dependable, but now she would cancel weekends with Greg and Laura half an hour before they were to go, and often didn't see them for weeks at a time. It's a busy time with a new baby, Mom would explain to Laura and Greg, but Meaghan could tell even Mom didn't believe that.

The porch door slammed and Meaghan raised her head to see Evan coming across the lawn. She sat up in the hammock. There must have been one of those programs on television last night on how to parent your teen. She wasn't used to all this attention.

"So how are things between you and Laura?" he asked.

Meaghan looked up at him. What was she supposed to say. Tell him his daughter was a jerk?

"That good, uh."

He didn't say anything more but wrapped his long arms around Meaghan. Omigosh, she was going to suffocate in here, but oddly enough she didn't mind. She was so tired, it felt kind of good to have someone big and solid to lean on.

"Evan, do you know the definition of the word air-conditioning?"

She could feel his laugh rumble deep in his chest.

CHAPTER 7

"You two back already? You just left." Meaghan's mother set the iron on end and smoothed a shirt sleeve with her hand.

"Meaghan doesn't like the woods," Greg complained. "She wanted to come back."

"It's too hot to be running around all those trees," Meaghan said. She stuck her head in the fridge to avoid Mom's eyes. Mom always said she could read Meaghan's face like a book and right about now, it had LIE printed across it in large, black letters. Except, Meaghan told herself, it wasn't really a lie—it was too hot. She poured a glass of milk and leaned against the refrigerator door.

"I thought it would be cooler in the shade," her mother said. Meaghan lifted the glass to her mouth, hoping it covered her face. It was useless trying to pull one over on Mom. Only, Meaghan shot a quick look at Greg, please don't let her say anything. Not in front of him. She didn't want to seem stupid to a ten year old.

How to explain to him that the dark, shadowy woods made her palms sweat. That the trees grew too thick and close together, and the lack of sunlight made it hard for her to breathe. She couldn't explain it to herself, let alone to Greg. *Yet you like the oaks and maples that shelter Miss Sarah's cottage. That's different, they seem safe somehow.*

It was late Monday morning, the beginning of the second

week of July. For the past month the sun had relentlessly leeched the colour from the trees, fields, and sky, leaving a tired, scorched blandness in its stead.

"Well, that's enough ironing. I'm dying of heat and besides which," Meaghan's mother snapped the board shut, "I detest doing it." She carried the iron into the laundry room. "I have some errands to do in the city. Do you two want to come?"

"I do." Meaghan asked. "I want to go to the main library."

"I'll drop you off there if you take Greg with you. I've quite a bit of running around to do, and I can do it a lot faster on my own. We'll meet for lunch afterwards," she promised.

"All right," Meaghan agreed.

Meaghan's mother eased the pickup out of the steep driveway onto the road.

"I'm not looking forward to going up that in the winter," she said.

How on earth could Mom even think about cold and snow in this heat, Meaghan wondered. She wiped the sweat from her forehead on the bottom of her T-shirt. And why were they in Evan's pickup? He was the one who constantly harped on the evils of air-conditioning, yet he was driving around in the cool comfort of Mom's car, while they cooked in his truck. She stuck her head out the window, then pulled it back in.

"Go faster, Mom," she demanded. Her mother drove so slow she didn't even stir up a gentle breeze. Still, wind or not, outside was preferable to the stifling interior of the truck.

Meaghan turned to stick her head out the window again, when she caught sight of a splash of purple against a backdrop of green and brown. Miss Sarah was working in her garden.

Meaghan raised her shoulders to her ears, lowered her head, and slid down the vinyl seat. *You look like a turtle—head in, head out—hiding in your shell.*

Meaghan squirmed uneasily. Why couldn't Mom just speed down the road like everyone else. Then maybe Miss Sarah wouldn't see her. She hadn't visited the old woman lately, well, since the day of her weird dream. It was just...the dream had made her feel strange and frightened, mostly of herself. Somehow she felt Miss Sarah was linked to that dream.

And that was what it had been—a dream brought on by the heat, the red pickup truck, and Miss Sarah's talk. Meaghan had been able to rationalize her torn fingers—gardening; the thin, red scratches on her arms—thorns from the woods; everything could be explained—except for the occasional melding of her world with a past one.

The first time it had happened she had been standing on the small hill behind their barn, watching Mr. Crawford drive a tractor around his field. Suddenly, she was looking down on a white blanket of cotton, dotted here and there with bent, black backs. The sound of soft singing and the air-splitting crack of a whip had carried to where she stood. Then she'd blinked and Mr. Crawford's tractor was once again moving below. *And Joshua. I'd forgotten all about him. Get real! Admit it, you see him at times as plain as the nose on your face. But he's not real, just a dreamed someone. He stroked your hair and told you it was pretty. And he sat next to you and you told him about Dad.*

The truck hit a pothole and Meaghan fell against Greg. She peeled her damp leg off his. The kid was like a furnace. Good thing he was sitting in the middle; she would never have survived the drive.

Meaghan and Greg climbed the flat, wide steps to the glass double doors leading into the library. She grunted and leaned all her weight against the handle. Why did they make the doors so heavy. Didn't they want people getting in? Cool air rushed out, slamming against the heat. Meaghan stood a moment before moving into the building, enjoying the shiver and prickle of goose bumps rising on her arms. Greg pushed her aside and headed down the stairs to the children's library.

"Turn right at the bottom," Meaghan called.

Greg's face looked up from the bend in the stairs. "I've been here before," he said.

Meaghan winced. He was right, he'd been here lots of times, while this was only her third visit. "Okay, sorry. I'll come and get you in an hour."

She watched Greg clatter down the stairs, then she went into the main library. She stopped in front of the long counter and read the various signs: the reference books were on the second floor. She walked up the stairs appreciatively sniffing the air. Books sure smelled great—musty, papery...booky. Joshua and Lanny would never know this smell.

She found an empty computer terminal and hit the space bar. "Any Word" it prompted and she began her search. After a few minutes, she walked between the tall shelves, hunting for information on slavery and the Underground Railroad. She leafed through a dozen books, then chose four that looked the most promising. She carried them to a long wooden table, sat down and opened the cover of the first book.

Lieutenant-Governor John Graves Simcoe of Upper Canada was one of the first people to work toward an anti-slavery law, she read. Skimming the page further, she found out that Simcoe did not free anyone presently in slavery, but gave any child born to a slave freedom at age twenty-five. That was old! Joshua would never have waited that long.

In 1777, Meaghan continued reading, *states north of the Mason-Dixon Line began to abolish slavery, but the southern states depended on slavery as cheap labour to work their large farms and plantations.*

Meaghan opened another book. It was about the Underground Railroad and she began reading. The Underground Railroad, she discovered, was formed in great secrecy around 1830, borrowing its name from real railroads. Like real railroads it moved people from one place to another, though in this case the passengers were slaves being moved from slavery to freedom.

The runaways were called "freight or packages," hiding places were "depots or stations," the people helping escaped slaves move from place to place were "conductors," and the organizers of the Underground Railroad were called "agents or stationmasters." Meaghan studied maps of the slave routes, trying to figure out where Joshua and Lanny lived in South Carolina, and the most likely route they would probably have followed to get to Canada. After a while, she closed the book and checked her watch. In fifteen minutes she would have to find Greg.

She pulled the last book toward her; *The Narratives of Fugitive Slaves in Canada* by Benjamin Drew. It was a book of interviews of actual slaves as they arrived in Canada, and it was ancient, first published in 1856.

Meaghan held the book in her hands, staring at it. It had been 1849 when Meaghan was there. If Lanny and Joshua had escaped, it was possible they could be in this book. *I thought you had decided it was a dream. Dreamed people wouldn't be in books. Put it back on the shelf; it's a waste of time. Reading and learning is never a waste of time, Joshua believed that. The dream guy?*

Keeping the book by Benjamin Drew to one side, Meaghan put the other three away. She would read it carefully, searching for a clue, anything that would tell her Joshua had been real.

She hurried down the steps to the children's library. Greg was sitting at a table watching a hamster running on a wire wheel. She plopped down on the chair next to Greg and watched the wheel turn round and round, powered by furiously working tiny feet.

"Do you think he knows he's not going anywhere?" Meaghan asked Greg. She watched a few minutes then laughed. "Have you ever seen anything so stupid?"

Greg grinned at her. "Yeah, you." He punched her arm. "You just sat here for five minutes watching the wheel go around."

"Can't you tell me something without hitting me. Geez." Meaghan rubbed her shoulder. The kid was solid. Suddenly she leapt up, her chair falling to the floor with a bang. She could see him, right there sitting next to Greg. She could see the small, thin figure of a boy–Daniel. Then he was gone. Meaghan put a hand to her forehead. This was getting too strange. Her brain was fried or something.

"You okay?" Greg asked. He was looking at her with an odd expression on his face.

"Uh...yeah, fine. Just clumsy." She spoke loudly, trying to appear casual in front of the watching kids. Just a clumsy girl knocking over a chair, that's all. She lowered her voice and whispered to Greg. "Did you just see a kid sitting there?" She pointed to the empty chair on the other side of him.

"No." He still had that peculiar look on his face.

Meaghan sighed. Even the stupid hamster had stopped running to watch her. "We'd better go. Mom'll be looking for us."

They had left the heavy city traffic and her mother had finally picked up speed on the county road. Meaghan hung her head out the window and lifted her hair from her neck. She wasn't going to think about the library, she was going to think about...her hair and the perpetual question—should she have it cut? It was hot, heavy, and unmanageable in this humidity. *Been wondering what this felt like all day long. Never been this close to such long hair. It feels pretty.* She'd put up with it.

"Want to stop for a video?" Meaghan's mother asked. They were approaching the town.

"Yeah!" Greg yelled. He bounced on the seat as they pulled into the store.

Meaghan left Greg and her mother to choose a movie and wandered over to the cooler. She opened the sliding door and stuck her head in, pretending to look at the different flavours of popsicles. It was really the cold she wanted, cold on her hot face. She sensed movement behind her, looked through the cooler's glass side and saw a man's shoe. *Dust covered brown boots, stitching working loose at the seams.* It was the store manager. Meaghan grabbed a grape freezee and shut the lid.

She wandered out to the front of the store and sat on the curb, waiting for Greg and her mother. Three men and Brad stood in a circle, talking and scuffing at the dirt with heavy workboots.

"Driest spring I've ever known. Wasn't even worth planting. Everything's going to shrivel up anyway if we don't get some rain," grumbled one man.

The others grunted their agreement.

"Except Sarah Johnston's place," a second man said. "Her land must be blessed or something. Drove by there the other day. Everything's green as green can be. Can't figure it out. As I said, must be blessed."

"Or we're cursed." Meaghan's head jerked up. She hadn't really been listening, so she couldn't tell which man had spoken. There was a snort of amusement from a couple of the men as they made their way to their trucks. Only Brad remained, and he was staring hard at Meaghan.

She couldn't tear her eyes from his gaze. It was such a cold and unfriendly stare that Meaghan felt increasingly uncomfortable. Why was he looking at her like that? She didn't even know him. Unless...that must be it. Laura had been telling him things about her, probably told him that Meaghan was a squealer. Even so, he didn't need to stare so much.

She heard the store door bang open and was relieved to see Greg and her mother. Brad looked at Meaghan a moment longer, then climbed into his red pickup and pulled away, tires spitting dust and gravel.

"Who was that boy?" Meaghan's mother asked. They climbed into Evan's truck. Meaghan yelped. The metal part of the seatbelt had burned her hand.

"That's Laura's boyfriend," Greg said.

"Laura's boyfriend?" Meaghan's mother started the truck's engine but didn't drive away. She stared after the red pickup. "He's a bit old for Laura, isn't he? What grade is he in?"

Meaghan shrugged. "I think he graduated this year. Why are you asking me? Ask Laura. I don't keep track of her social life." Though she probably could, Meaghan thought. She didn't exactly have one of her own to keep her occupied.

Meaghan's mother backed the truck away from the store, absently shifted into first gear, and headed down the road toward the farmhouse. Her forehead was creased by two deep lines and one corner of her mouth was turned up, the other down. Meaghan knew those signs. Mom was worried and she wasn't very happy. Laura was certainly causing Mom a lot of trouble.

Meaghan was beginning to feel cheerful. Maybe it wasn't so bad having a stepsister around. It kind of took the pressure off having one's own behaviour scrutinized all the time. Compared to Laura, Meaghan was an angel these days–a dull, boring angel.

They inched up the driveway and turned into the garage at the back of the house.

"Oh no," Meaghan's mother said softly. "Now what." A police car was parked in front of the kitchen door.

CHAPTER 8

"Get back in here, now!"

The police car was going down the driveway and Laura was sidling up the stairs when Meaghan's mother's voice sliced the air. Laura stopped and stood on the bottom step. Meaghan could tell the other girl was trying to look casual and slightly bored, and it would have been pretty believable if that tiny pulse in Laura's neck wasn't beating so rapidly.

While her mother was speaking to the police, Meaghan had watched with fascination the red climb from her mother's neck, flood into her cheeks and forehead, then spread flames into her already fiery hair. Mom was ready to burst.

"Wow!" Greg's eyes were bulging.

"You ain't seen nothing yet, kid," Meaghan whispered. "Mom's Irish and she has red hair." It was gratifying to see someone else on the receiving end of her mother's anger for a change.

"Meaghan, you and Greg go outside."

Meaghan shuffled to the kitchen door and stopped, hoping her mother wouldn't notice.

"Now!" She had noticed. Meaghan and Greg rushed out the door. Greg started down the steps, but Meaghan grabbed him by the arm.

"Sit down," she hissed. "I want to listen."

"But she said to go outside."

"Mom didn't say exactly how far outside. And this,"

Meaghan waved an arm around the porch, "certainly qualifies as outside."

Meaghan sat down on the porch floor by the kitchen door. Greg hesitated a moment, then shrugged and sat beside her.

"I hope you're right," he said. "Because if I get in trouble, I'm going to say you're older and you told me to."

"Fine, fine," Meaghan hissed. "Now be quiet, I don't want to miss any of this." It was a great spot; she could hear Mom loud and clear.

"You were supposed to be at your mother's. Why weren't you there."

"Mom called just after you left and said she couldn't pick me up after all. The baby was sick or something," Laura said. "I didn't do anything. I wasn't throwing rocks."

"But you were there."

"Well...yeah, but I didn't..."

"I don't care if you threw a rock or not," Meaghan's mother interrupted Laura. "You were there and that's the issue. Whether or not you threw a rock doesn't matter. Just by being there, being with these kids, you were in the wrong. You condoned their actions. You might as well have thrown a rock."

Meaghan could hear her mother take a deep breath in an attempt to control her anger. "Three of Miss Sarah's windows were broken. What if one of those rocks had hit her, or if she had been cut by flying glass. Did you think of that for one minute?"

Meaghan heard Laura mumble but couldn't make out what she said. She had no trouble hearing her mother.

"Get it through your thick head!" Mom's forced calm was short-lived. "It doesn't matter whether or not you actually threw a rock. It doesn't make you any less to blame. You didn't stop them from attacking Miss Sarah."

"They didn't attack her." That was better, Meaghan thought. Laura was yelling now.

"They broke her windows, destroyed property. I consider that an attack, don't you? She's an elderly woman. This could have ended very differently. The police told me Miss Sarah is not pressing charges. But don't imagine for one moment you are getting off easy here, because you aren't. Because I also know that this isn't the first time these kids have harassed Miss Sarah, and you know it too. Well, it stops now. You are not to see them again, especially Brad. No fourteen-year-old girl should be running around in pickup trucks, hanging out with older kids, getting into who knows what kind of trouble."

"You can't tell me what to do. You're not my mother," Laura shouted.

"You live in my house, you follow my rules."

"Your house! It's Dad's house and mine and Greg's, not yours. You and Meaghan just move in and you figure it's yours?"

"It is my house. I am your father's wife, now and always, and you are going to have to accept that. Your attitude stinks. We've been tiptoeing around here, trying to give you time, making excuses for your rude behaviour. Well, I've had enough. I will not have a spoiled brat like you making everyone in this house miserable. Keep you mouth shut when I am talking!"

Greg snickered behind his hand. Meaghan poked him in the ribs.

"We might as well get another thing straight. My name is Sharon. Not you, she, or her, but Sharon. Or if you don't like my name, you may call me Mrs. Somter. I am also not your personal slave. You will help out with housework and yard work and anything else your father and I ask you to do."

"What are you two doing?"

Meaghan's heart nearly burst through her ribs. She and Greg had been so intent on the argument raging inside they hadn't heard Evan come up behind them.

"Mom told us to stay outside." Meaghan widened her green eyes. She had practiced long hours in front of her mirror to perfect this innocent look. Still, Mom never fell for it.

Evan walked to the kitchen door and listened for a moment, then turned back to them.

"And this is as far outside as you two got," he said. He grinned wryly at Meaghan. Obviously he was familiar with innocent looks. He reached into his pocket and took out some change. "Bike down to the store and get yourselves a popsicle."

"I just had one," Meaghan said.

"Well, have another." Evan pushed open the screen door. "And take your time."

Supper was a hastily thrown together, subdued affair. An unhappy looking Laura pushed a few peas around her plate; Meaghan's mother sighed every few minutes and Evan was silent and thoughtful. Meaghan watched Greg shovel food into his mouth. It was disgusting the way that kid ate. He had inhaled his entire supper.

Meaghan averted her eyes, staring at her own full plate. She just wanted to be far away from them all. This wasn't anything like the joyous family dinners she had seen on television. There should be a law about showing fantasy to kids.

She escaped the house as soon as she could and was surprised to find her feet taking her toward Miss Sarah's cottage. She jumped a mile when Laura stepped out from behind a tree trunk, and stood in the middle of the road waiting for her.

Meaghan looked apprehensively at the other girl. She didn't think Laura was prone to violence, but for some people those were famous last words.

"What are you doing here?" Meaghan asked.

"Dad and...," Laura hesitated a moment, "...Sharon said I had to apologize to Miss Sarah."

Laura looked so miserable that Meaghan almost felt sorry for her. But not quite. She took a closer look at the other girl. There was something different about her. Her face was scrubbed bare, and her lips were pink instead of red. Laura looked like a kid again, just like Meaghan. Funny, she had never noticed before, but she and Laura were the exact same height. It had always seemed to Meaghan that Laura was taller.

"You have this strange habit," Laura said. "You stare at people. It's real weird."

Do I do that? Do I stare at people? We've been meaning to talk to you about that. You're still staring. She's just curious, interested in people.

"What are you doing here?" Laura asked.

"I was going to see Miss Sarah, but if you're going down you probably don't want me there. Unless of course, you want me to come with you?" Meaghan asked eagerly. *You are so transparent. You are dying to see Laura apologize to Miss Sarah. She's just trying to be friendly and supportive. Friendly, my ass. The girl is warped.*

Laura shrugged. "I don't care." They walked together down the lane.

"So," Laura said suddenly. "I guess you've been doing quite a bit of squealing on me."

Meaghan thought hard for a moment. *Deny it. Widen your eyes, use your innocent face. Always tell the truth, you'll find it easier in the long run. She'll probably pound you out right here.*

"I told about you being in the pickup truck that day. I didn't know about rocks and windows," Meaghan said. They were standing in front of the gate to the yellow cottage. "You won't believe me, but I didn't tell Mom just to get you in trouble. Miss Sarah is my friend, and I felt really bad that she was hurt. I told Mom because...well, I've always told her everything." *Almost everything.*

Laura didn't reply. She was looking nervously at Miss Sarah's house.

"She's not a witch, you know," Meaghan said

"But she is different," Laura replied. "Normal people don't do their gardening during the witching hours."

"Laura, in case you haven't noticed, it's been real hot during the day lately, and Miss Sarah gardens at night because it's cooler. That's all, no great mystery."

"Yeah, right. You were the one jumping around the bedroom in the middle of the night, scared to death," Laura pointed out.

Meaghan grinned sheepishly.

"Why do you come down here all the time?" Laura asked.

Meaghan looked suspiciously at the other girl, but she seemed genuinely curious.

"I like her house and I like her garden. Imagine me, a city kid, liking gardens. I also like Miss Sarah." Meaghan groped for words to explain how she felt when she visited the yellow cottage. "She's a peaceful person to be around." Inadequate, but the best she could do.

"Not like me," Laura said. Her mouth quirked up in an unexpected smile. *She really has a beautiful face. It looks even better without all that gunk. Rats! Rats! Rats! I want to be her.*

"Well," Meaghan said. "I'm not the most peaceful person to be around either. Mom says I can be as prickly as a porcupine at times."

Laura grinned again and pushed open the gate and walked to the blue door. Meaghan followed slowly. She didn't believe it. She and Laura had actually had a conversation that hadn't ended in a flurry of insults.

Miss Sarah opened the door not seeming the least bit surprised to see them. Meaghan noticed three glasses and a pitcher of lemonade sitting on the small porch table. She looked up and caught Laura's eyes. She had seen the preparations, too. Meaghan lifted her shoulders in a small shrug and perched on the edge of a wicker chair. Laura remained standing, shifting awkwardly from one foot to the other.

"Miss Sarah," Laura began. She was watching the toe of her shoe run along a crack in the floor. All of a sudden Meaghan remembered the apology scene in *Anne of Green Gables*. Anne had fallen to her knees and apologized profusely and dramatically to Mrs. Lynde. Meaghan looked at Laura hopefully. It would be quite exciting if Laura suddenly dropped to her knees, but highly unlikely.

"Miss Sarah," Laura started again. "I'm really sorry about your windows. I didn't throw any rocks myself, but I understand that by being there it was as bad as if I had thrown rocks."

Miss Sarah's chair moved back and forth, but she said nothing.

Laura stumbled on. "And I'm sorry about the other afternoon, you know, when the red truck and...all those things that were said. I really am sorry." Laura's voice trailed off.

Not as entertaining as Anne Shirley, Meaghan thought, but Laura did have a certain sincerity.

Miss Sarah stood up and nodded her head at Laura. "I accept your apology. Now you sit down there next to Meaghan and we'll have some lemonade."

Meaghan was surprised to see Laura's hand shaking slightly as she took a glass from Miss Sarah. Laura had been scared and upset, Meaghan realized. Could it be that she really was sorry? For a moment, Meaghan almost...*liked* Laura.

Miss Sarah sat down with a small groan. "Been doing too much work in my garden. I'm getting stiff. You haven't been down to see me much lately, Meaghan. Been too busy I expect." Meaghan slurped her lemonade loudly, clinking the ice in her glass. Miss Sarah smiled and turned to Laura. "Your Dad brought me some more straw and grass clippings this afternoon."

"What for?" Laura asked.

"I've been putting them around the plants. In hot weather it helps to keep moisture in the ground.

Blessed garden, indeed, Meaghan thought. Hard work kept that garden green.

"Your Dad said I could count on your help the next couple of days, spreading the last of the straw and grass."

"He did?" Laura's eyebrows nearly disappeared under the fringe of hair.

Meaghan sat back happily in her chair. That would be a messy, hot job.

"He offered Meaghan's help too." Miss Sarah's wide, toothy smile flashed at Meaghan. "More hands make light work."

The porch door slammed back against the wall with a bang and Moses slunk in, his huge head moving slyly side to side. Meaghan pulled her feet far under her chair and looked about for a handy weapon to protect herself, but Moses passed her and jumped into Miss Sarah's lap. He lay there purring and docile.

Miss Sarah absently stroked the orange fur. "I haven't seen you for quite a while, Laura. When you were a little thing your mama used to bring you to see me quite often."

"She did?"

"Sat right there on that chair where you're sitting, with you on her knee, all gussied up in beautiful, frilly dresses."

Laura looked down at the chair as if she could find a piece of her mother still there.

"She was so proud of you."

"Not any more." Laura gave a short laugh and turned her head away, but not before Meaghan saw the shine of tears. "She just cares about her new family now."

"She cares. She forgot to show it lately, is all," Miss Sarah said. "Sometimes it happens that people's lives get off track and they flounder around a bit looking for the way back on. That's what's happening to your mama right now. Give her a little time and I expect things will work out. You're a bit off track yourself at the moment, but I have every faith that you'll be back on soon." Miss Sarah was quiet for a few minutes.

"I spoke to Meaghan's mother this afternoon," she said. "Seems a really nice lady."

Meaghan watched the shadows of the oaks deepen and

stretch across Miss Sarah's yard. Darkness pooled in the corners of the porch. Even as Meaghan watched, they spread, a creeping blackness, to where Laura sat unmoving, her face mask hard, eyes fixed on some distant point.

Move! Meaghan wanted to shout at her. Do something! Don't you see! You're letting the blackness in! But she sat silent, listening to the rhythmic squeak of Miss Sarah's rocking chair and the early cries of the night birds.

CHAPTER 9

Meaghan lifted an armful of straw and grass clippings from the wheelbarrow and threw it on the dirt between two rows of beans. She had been right—this was a hot, messy job. Dead grass was sticking to her legs and arms, making her body one big itch. Maybe she could pretend to be allergic to the straw, fake some sneezes; except no one would believe her.

She looked over to where Laura was bent at the waist, half-heartedly spreading the mixture of straw and grass. Meaghan blinked rapidly. It was as though a gauzy, grey veil had been suddenly drawn over the other girl.

She could see Laura's blue-jean shorts and T-shirt, yet superimposed over these was the distinct outline of a loose, brown shift. The straw and grass clippings beneath Laura's feet were stirred up into yellow dust, and on each side of where Laura stood was a row of rude, wooden shacks. *Fragments of whispers and secrets lingering on the sun-heated air.*

But why Laura? After all, it wasn't her dream. Meaghan anxiously chewed the inside of her lip, watching the other girl bend and straighten as she worked through the constantly wavering landscape. It was getting worse! The blending of her time with one that was past was happening more frequently. What if she became unable to separate the two?

"You're doing it again," Laura said.

"What?"

"Staring at me." Laura leaned against the wheelbarrow. "I need a break. And a drink."

Meaghan followed her to the edge of Miss Sarah's garden and flung herself under the nearest tree. Laura poured water from the thermos into a glass, then passed the thermos to Meaghan.

"It's been a great summer vacation so far," she said. "Killing myself working in a garden, thanks to you."

"Thanks to me!" Meaghan spluttered. "I didn't do anything. In fact, you get in trouble and I end up being punished. I don't even know why I have to be here."

"Because my dad and your mom think we should spend more time together. That way, they hope, we'll eventually become friends."

"Fat chance," said Meaghan. "We sleep in the same room every night. Isn't that enough together?" She shredded a leaf between her fingers. "Besides, why can't we be together at the movies or the mall, instead of here."

"Because I'm grounded for life, remember?" Laura absently picked up the book that Meaghan had brought with her. "*Narratives of Fugitive Slaves in Canada,*" she read out loud. "Looks real interesting." She rolled her eyes and flipped through the pages. "How can you read this stuff? Look how small the print is."

Meaghan reached over and grabbed the book from Laura's hand. "The last thing you probably read was by Dr. Seuss—big print and lots of pictures."

She dropped the book in her lap, then glared down at it. She didn't want to read it. In fact, she blamed it for all the strange stuff that had been happening to her lately; yet she had to finish it, because somewhere in that small print there might be something of Joshua.

Laura stood up and Meaghan watched her gracefully stretch her arms above her head. "Give yourself time," Mom had said.

"Don't rush growing up." She could live to be a hundred years old and she'd never have a body like Laura's.

"Well, I guess we slaves better get back to work," Laura groaned.

"Slaves!" Meaghan jumped to her feet. "You don't have a clue what it's like to be a slave. Never having enough to eat, always being tired and dirty, having someone change your name if they feel like it, taking your family away, and never ever belonging to yourself! You got it so good. Just ask Miss Sarah. Her great-grandmother was a slave. She'll tell you what it was like!" Meaghan shouted.

"You better quit reading that book. It's affecting your brain," Laura said.

"Well, at least I have one to be affected."

"Girls, there's some lunch at the house for you." Meaghan whirled about to find Miss Sarah standing beside her.

Meaghan held her book tightly to her chest as she followed Miss Sarah to the yellow cottage, then stopped so abruptly that Laura crashed into her. *What was it Laura had said? Mom and Evan were trying to get her and Laura together more.*

"Move!" Laura shoved her from behind and Meaghan stumbled forward. *Could it actually be working? True, they were fighting, but still...they were, what's the word, interacting. Omigosh! Mom being right on her own was a big pain, but Evan and Mom together was going to be downright unbearable.*

"You girls come right in, wash and tidy yourselves," Miss Sarah said. Meaghan passed through the tiny living room into the kitchen.

"Are you going somewhere, Miss Sarah?" asked Laura. "I saw a suitcase in the other room."

Meaghan ran hot water into the sink and soaped her hands. The green stains on them would never go away no matter how hard she scrubbed.

"Yes, I am, Laura," said Miss Sarah. "I'm going away for a few days and was going to ask you girls if you could take care of Moses for me. He pines terribly when left alone, and I know he would enjoy your company. I spoke to your mother, Meaghan, and she said it was all right with her."

"Sure," Laura agreed.

Meaghan turned from the sink and threw a towel at Laura.

"Well, thank you. One less thing to worry about." Miss Sarah was scratching the underside of Moses' chin. The orange cat purred in loud, low brrrps. "You two go sit on the porch and I'll bring the sandwiches in a jiffy."

"What's your problem?" Laura asked as she led the way through the living room.

Meaghan jabbed her in the back. "Why'd you say we'd take that animal?"

"Well, why not?"

"Because it's the cat from hell," Meaghan hissed. She sat cautiously on the edge of a wicker chair, keeping a close watch on the door.

"He seems a nice enough animal," Laura said. "Do you have a cat phobia or something?"

"No, I don't have a cat phobia, just a Moses phobia. He's an absolute terror, vicious. You'll soon see." Meaghan drew her feet back under her chair. "Here he comes."

Moses wandered into the porch. Laura gave Meaghan a pitying look and held out her hand to the orange cat.

"Here kitty," she said. "Nice kitty."

Moses crouched, his stomach pressed against the porch floor. His ears flattened and orange fur puffed out as one taloned paw raked across Laura's outstretched hand. Laura shrieked and snatched back her hand. Moses growled and spat, moving menacingly toward Laura, backing her into a corner.

"Do something! Get it away from me!" Laura screeched. Meaghan watched with delight.

Miss Sarah hurried into the porch carrying a tray. "Moses," she scolded. "Are you being naughty?"

The cat sat demurely grooming himself as Laura edged back into her chair, nursing her hurt hand. She glared at Meaghan.

"So where are you going, Miss Sarah?" Meaghan asked. She reached for a sandwich. Boy, a little action sure made a person hungry.

"My nephew's wife is doing poorly, so it seems a good time to go see the family. They mostly all live in the Chatham area. Been family there for a hundred years and more."

"Meaghan's reading a book about slaves," Laura said. Her eyes were glued to Moses. "Your ancestors escaped on the Underground Railroad, I hear."

"That's right. My great-grandmother ran away one night in late August, 1849, from a plantation in South Carolina, and arrived in Canada early in the new year. She settled in the Raleigh Township area in a small community of escaped slaves. She brought my granddaddy with her. Although he was just a little boy of five then, said he'd always remember the wonderful people who helped them."

Miss Sarah lowered herself into her rocking hair. "First thing my great-grandmother did when she got here was learn to read and write. Went to school right along with my granddaddy and eventually taught school herself. Said education was the greatest joy of freedom. My granddaddy was also a school teacher, then my daddy and then me. Education was very important in our family." Miss Sarah wheezed and puffed a few moments, then went on.

"But, you know, my granddaddy and my father, and even myself for a little while, could only teach in a black school. White folks didn't want their children being taught alongside black children, especially by black teachers. Black people could live in Canada, and be free, as long as they didn't live too close to white people." Miss Sarah's lips stretched in her wide smile. *Joshua's smile.*

Meaghan had chewed her bread into a soggy lump, but her throat refused to open and let her swallow. "What was her name?" Meaghan asked. She finally forced the sandwich down. "Your great-grandmother's name?"

"Lanny. Her name was Lanny Johnston, and my granddaddy was Daniel Johnston."

Meaghan couldn't breathe. Her lungs were hurting like crazy. "What about Joshua?" she asked. "You didn't say anything about Joshua."

Somehow she knew that what Miss Sarah would tell her was going to be awful, but not knowing was worse.

"Who's Joshua?" Laura asked.

Miss Sarah didn't seem to find Meaghan's question unusual.

"Joshua was my granddaddy's older brother. He ran away the same time they did, but he didn't make it to Canada. My granddaddy always said that was his mother's greatest sorrow, not knowing whatever happened to him–if he lived to be old, or died young, where he was buried."

Her lungs were bursting. She had to get air, or she was going to faint. Meaghan stood up and started for the door.

"Just a minute, Meaghan. I'll get Moses' things." Miss Sarah bustled out of the porch soon returning with an empty wire cage and a plastic bag. She looped the bag over Meaghan's wrist, then opened the door of the cage and wrestled the cat in head first, tucking in stray bits of fur before fastening the door. She handed it to Laura who reluctantly took the cage, holding it carefully away from her body.

Miss Sarah chuckled. "He's a handful at times, but once he gets to know you, he's your friend forever."

"Great," said Laura. She held the cage out farther.

"Now, I'll be back in three days. Friday afternoon to be exact," said Miss Sarah. "Enough time to see everyone, but not wear out my welcome. That bag you have, Meaghan, is Moses' cat food and a blanket he's quite fond of. Laura's father is going to keep an eye on the house for me and you have the cat and I guess that's everything. My ride will be here soon so I better get my hat on."

Meaghan found herself out the door and at the bottom of the wooden steps, without any memory of getting there.

"I hope you have a nice trip," Laura said.

Meaghan walked down the path to the gate and out to the lane.

"Wait up!" Laura called.

Meaghan kept on walking and Laura panted up beside her.

"What's the matter with you?" Laura asked. "You didn't even say goodbye."

"Nothing's wrong," Meaghan said. *Why fight it? You're going, going, gone crazy. They're coming to take you away, away. Mom would feel bad, but Laura would have her room to herself again, and Meaghan would have her own room too, a nice padded one.*

"Here, you take him, he weighs a ton." Laura shoved the cage into Meaghan's hands, and took the plastic bag. She held out her hand to show Meaghan the angry, red lines. "You could have warned me about him."

Meaghan opened her mouth, then snapped it shut. She had more pressing matters to think about. She automatically moved out of reach of one flailing paw and continued walking.

The only other explanation to her being nuts was that it had actually happened. She had gone back in time, which, with all the supporting evidence she had, was beginning to seem more and more likely. It couldn't be a coincidence that she knew their names—Joshua, Lanny, and Daniel—that they were from South Carolina and had left in 1849. The crackle of plastic distracted Meaghan. Laura was rummaging around in the bag she carried.

"Look at this stuff," Laura said. "*Gourmet Dinner, Beef Wellington, Seafood Supreme*. Like cats can read labels, or even care." She dropped the can she was holding into the bag and searched deeper.

"What's this?" A flash of silver cut across Meaghan's vision, blinding her momentarily, but not before she saw the small tin Laura was shaking. Something inside it banged against the metal sides. "I wonder what's in here," Laura said.

"Don't open that!" Meaghan's hand let go of the handle of the cat cage and it fell with a thud onto the road. Moses began a piercing yowling. Meaghan grabbed Laura's elbow, but it was too late. Laura had already pried the top open with one perfect, red-tipped nail and was peering inside.

CHAPTER 10

Black! Black all around her, filling her eyes, so Meaghan couldn't tell if she was up, down, or sideways. Her heart beat thunderously in her ears. Her jaws were achingly clenched, and her hands were bunched in tight fists. Death was black. The clothes, the hearse, the piled earth, the yawning black hole that had swallowed Dad. Dad lost forever in the black, and now it wanted her. *Voices where are you? Are you dead, too?*

Meaghan thrust her arm forward and grazed her knuckles on the rough bark of a tree. The pain was familiar and comforting. She wouldn't feel pain if she were dead, would she?

As her rapid breathing eased she heard a faint rustle of cloth, the scuff of a foot on dry leaves, a stirring of the air about her, and a child's whimper quickly stilled. There were people here.

With the return of her hearing Meaghan's other senses flooded back. A dank, moist odor stung her nose. Her mouth tasted of rust and metal. She had read somewhere about the stink of fear. Well, this must be how it tastes.

White-rimmed eyes loomed out of the dark close to her face. Meaghan started in terror and her heart, just beginning to quiet, pounded violently again.

"Meaghan?" It was just a breathing of her name, but she recognized the voice.

"Lanny?" Meaghan's eyes were slowly adjusting to the dark. She could now see the dim outline of a woman's body crouched next to her and a smaller figure lying in a ball at the woman's feet. Daniel! She was back in South Carolina. Back in 1849.

There was movement beyond Lanny's shoulders. Another pair of eyes peered at Meaghan, these light blue and rounded in terror.

"Laura!" Meaghan spoke aloud in her surprise. What was Laura doing here?

"Hush," Lanny hissed, then she drew in a sharp breath and touched Meaghan's arm. Someone was coming through the brush toward them.

Lanny and Daniel melted into the bushes, disappearing so silently and completely Meaghan wondered if they had really been there.

Icy fingers encircled her ankle. Meaghan gasped and tried to jerk her leg free, then realized the hand was Laura's. She turned to speak to the other girl, when she heard again the sound of leaves being pushed aside but closer now.

Meaghan crawled into the shadow of a stump, pulling Laura beside her, then pushing her into the deeper darkness. She wished she had something to hide Laura's blonde curls and dampen the pale light that seemed to radiate from her blue eyes. They waited silently.

"Mama? Where you gone to?" It was Joshua. Meaghan felt relief surge through her, leaving her giddy and weak in its wake. Joshua was safe. They crept from their hiding places and gathered around him.

"No one's followin' us yet, Mama, but it's best we go through the swamp. Goin' 'round will take too long." His voice was low and Meaghan moved closer to hear him. "I want to be as far away from the house as we can come mornin'. We better get movin'."

Joshua picked up Daniel and began to walk into the wall of black that was the beginning of the swamp. Lanny followed.

Meaghan's feet were rooted to the spot where she stood. She could feel the black searching for her, reaching out decaying, stinking tendrils to pull her into the swamp. She couldn't do it. She couldn't follow Lanny and Joshua into that dark. If only there was a light of some sort.

Meaghan looked up through tangled branches and saw the white ghost ring around the edges of a new moon. There was no help there. She wanted to be home, her real home, the apartment in Toronto; not the farmhouse on top of the hill. Why had she come back to this place? What was she doing here?

"Meaghan?" Laura's fingers dug into Meaghan's arm.

Meaghan gestured to her to be quiet. She didn't have much time to think this out, and it was difficult getting her brain to work with the blackness crowding her mind. She had to figure out how to get back to her own time, right now. She was not going into that swamp.

Meaghan thought furiously. There had been two common threads throughout this whole thing—Miss Sarah and...the tin box. Every time she peered into that box, she went somewhere. Meaghan's eyes widened. Chances were that right now Joshua and Lanny were carrying it into the swamp. She was going to have to go in or never get home.

○ ○ ○ ○ ○

Meaghan had never been so tired. Mud seeped between her toes and sucked at her ankles, making every step agony. At first she had tried to avoid the stumps and roots, but it made the

going too slow. She was terrified that she would fall behind and be lost in the swamp. Meaghan concentrated on Lanny's back, trying to ignore the slithering and scuttling sounds about her, the constant insect drone, the delicate brushing against her face, and the occasional harsh cry from the surrounding swamp.

At times they would stop while Joshua tested the ground before them with a long stick. Then he would move on and Meaghan would follow, feeling his urgency infecting her as she put one foot in front of the other. Finally Joshua stopped to rest.

"Are you sure we aren't going around in circles?" Meaghan asked. The words came out slurred. Her mouth was too tired to shape vowels and consonants.

"I'm followin' the North Star," Joshua said. He pointed into the sky where a silver light hung low and bright. "That way I know we're goin' in one direction. I've been keepin' it in front of me. They say if you follow the North Star it'll lead you all the way to Canada." Joshua bent down and picked up a sleeping Daniel. "We better keep movin'. Good thing it's the dark of the moon, hide's us pretty good."

Dark of the moon. Plant by the dark of the moon. Run by the dark of the moon.

Meaghan searched through the web of vines and branches above her as she walked, and found the North Star. She stared at it, willing it into her mind. Joshua said you could follow it all the way to Canada. Well, she better know where it was just in case they got separated, then she'd be able to follow it home.

Grotesque, twisted shapes loomed on all sides of her as the

dark lightened to grey. Dawn was not far away now. She could no longer see the star.

"Gettin' light," Joshua said. "We'll have to stay put for the day, else we'll only go 'bout in circles with no star to guide us. This looks like as good a place as any to hole up."

He pointed to a large tree that had fallen, its roots forming an opening. Joshua cleared out dead leaves and animal droppings, and Lanny, Daniel, and Laura crawled in. Meaghan followed, shocked to see the swollen, cut soles of Laura's feet ahead of her. They had both been limping badly the last while, and Meaghan suspected her feet probably looked like Laura's, but she wasn't about to check. Probably better not to know.

In the dim light, she saw that Laura looked really bad, shaking and chilled; her eyes were glazed and dull. What worried Meaghan more was that Laura hadn't even questioned where she was, or what she was doing here. It was very unlike her.

Joshua pulled a branch in front of the opening. Laura, Daniel, and Lanny lay down and were instantly asleep. Meaghan stared at the root roof above her. *Better not think about the slugs and worms living there. It's kind of like being buried alive. Still, it's better than being caught by the overseer.*

The dirt ceiling seemed to be lower now. Meaghan couldn't lay there any longer. She sat up and saw Joshua peering out the opening. Meaghan was happy to see him awake. Talking to someone would help keep her mind, and those helpful voices, occupied.

"Joshua."

"I thought you'd be sleeping," Joshua said.

"Can't," Meaghan said shortly. She crawled over to sit beside him. "How big is this swamp?" she asked.

"Don't know," Joshua answered. "I heard that a man could cross it in a day, but I don't actually know anyone who ever did. If yo're runnin' away and you get through the swamp you don't come back to tell everybody how long it took you to do it."

Meaghan saw his white smile flash. Where did he get the strength to pull his lips into a grin?

"The ground though, don't seem so wet or soft here," he went on. "I think we might be comin' to the finish of it."

"So you're running away," Meaghan said. "Did something happen?"

She could see Joshua's puzzled expression in the grey light. She must sound kind of stupid; he seemed to think she should know everything. Did that mean she and Laura were here in 1849 all the time, or did they just pop in and out? Joshua and Lanny didn't seemed overly surprised to see them.

What was also odd was that they hadn't commented on Laura's blonde hair and blue eyes, definitely not the usual colouring of a field slave. Perhaps when they looked at Laura and her, Lanny and Joshua didn't see what she saw. Meaghan shivered.

"Slavetraders were comin'," Joshua said. "Harvest's almost done and master don't want to feed us all 'til plantin' season so he's sellin' some of us. Me, I'm a hard worker so I know I was staying, and Mama, she works hard too, up at the big house. It's mostly the young ones they was comin' for, young ones like Daniel. He's always been small for his years, but this time, well, I felt it in my bones, this time they'd take him." Joshua's voice broke.

"Only five years old and they'd take him from his Mama,"

Joshua whispered fiercely. "That's when I thought, no, we's people too, and we hurt when our family are taken away. I been scared too long to leave. But not any more."

Meaghan could think of nothing to say.

"I was sure glad to see you and Laura there with Mama. I didn't know if you'd be able to get away. You's too young, too much of your life ahead to live like that, being someone else's property. In Canada all men are free, nobody's owned by nobody. I remember my daddy always sayin' that."

"Joshua," Meaghan said suddenly. "What's your last name?"

"Johnston. Joshua Johnston."

...his mother's greatest sorrow—not knowing whatever happened to him, if he lived to be old, or died young, where he was buried.

Meaghan was terrified. If Joshua tried to escape to Canada, he'd be caught. But, if somehow she could convince him to go back to the plantation, would that change? Could history be changed?

"Joshua, you got to go back." Meaghan shook his arm.

"Go back? I just run away."

"But," how could she persuade him to return? "If you get caught, they'll beat you, maybe even kill you. Joshua, I don't want you dead!" Meaghan was still shaking his arm. *Don't want you dead, too!*

"I'm dead already workin' that plantation," Joshua said.

"No you're not. Dead is being lost in the black." Meaghan could hear the hysteria in her own voice but couldn't stop it.

"What do you mean?"

"Ever since my dad died, every time I talk about him, even think about him, it's like this great blackness comes, and it wants to take me, too. I think that's what it is when you're dead—a black nothing," Meaghan sobbed.

Joshua put an arm around her and held her tight. "Blackness is back there, on that plantation," he told her. "I never thought of death as black. I always believed it was light."

He gently pushed her from him. "Now, get some sleep, girl. We've a long piece to travel come nightfall." Joshua parted the branches and went out through the opening. "I'm gonna sit just outside here and keep watch."

Meaghan lay down beside Laura, thinking about what Joshua had said. He believed death was light. *Out of the darkness and into the light.*

"Meaghan?"

She had thought Laura was asleep.

"Meaghan, where are we? Who are these people? What did you do to me?" Laura was sounding more like herself.

"Why do you automatically blame me?" asked Meaghan. "It's your fault."

"My fault! I didn't do anything."

"You opened the tin box."

"What tin box?"

"The tin box in the bag Miss Sarah gave us. Remember the bag with the cat food?"

"A tin box! Why are you talking about a stupid tin box? I just want to know what's going on!" Laura's voice was shrill.

"It's hard to explain." That was the understatement of the year. "It happened to me once before," Meaghan said. "Miss Sarah showed me the box, and I opened it, and the next thing I knew I was on a plantation picking cotton. Joshua and Lanny were there."

"What is this, a dream?"

"Actually, we're back in time, 1849 to be exact, in South

Carolina." Saying the words made Meaghan realize she didn't even believe herself, so how on earth was Laura going to believe her.

"And we're slaves," she added quickly. May as well let Laura know everything at once.

"South Carolina! 1849!" Laura screeched. "Slaves!"

"Would you keep your voice down," Meaghan hissed. "You'll wake everyone up. Besides, there's slavehunters out there looking for us and your big mouth will lead them right here."

"Why are they looking for us?" Laura was still screeching.

"Be quiet," Meaghan whispered through clenched teeth. She was going to gag Laura in a moment if the other girl didn't shut up.

"They're hunting for us because we're escaped slaves. We belong to the guy who owns the plantation, and he wants us back."

"We don't belong to anyone. We can't be slaves. We're not even black." Laura was incredulous. "I have blonde hair and blue eyes. No one in their right mind would think I was a black person." At least she had lowered her voice a decibel or two.

"I don't think they see us like we see us," Meaghan said carefully.

"What do you mean?"

"I think Lanny or Joshua would have said something about your hair and eyes. But they didn't. I don't think they see them. I think here we look...black."

"Black!" Laura's voice climbed sharply again. "What do I look like to you?"

"I see you...as you." Meaghan felt like she was drowning in confusion. "They just don't see you...as you."

"I want to go home. Right now. Where's that box?" Laura demanded.

"I don't know. The last time I found it in Lanny's cabin, and I opened it and I was home. After that, Miss Sarah had it, then you. I don't know where the box is now." Meaghan felt close to tears. She was so tired.

"It's Miss Sarah, isn't it." Laura's eyes were shooting blue sparks. "She did this. I told you she was a witch and now she's sent us here."

"She's not a witch," Meaghan insisted. "But she is involved. I think Daniel is Miss Sarah's grandfather and Lanny is her great-grandmother."

"Find that box," Laura ordered.

"Lanny might have it in the bag she's carrying," Meaghan said.

"Well, look."

Meaghan gently loosened the cloth bag from Lanny's hand. The woman was so exhausted, Meaghan realized, she could whack her over the head and Lanny wouldn't wake up. Still she didn't want Joshua to hear. She felt around in the bag, but could not find anything hard and cold.

"Well?"

"There's nothing here. Maybe Lanny left the tin at the cabin."

Laura was reaching for Lanny's bag when the branches covering the door were swept aside and a hand reached through and grabbed Meaghan's arm.

"Get up! Get up! We gotta get out of here." Joshua was yelling and dragging her from the shelter. Laura crawled out, then Lanny, pushing Daniel before her.

"Master's got the dogs hunting us!"

CHAPTER 11

"Go that way!" Joshua pointed over Lanny's shoulder. "Keep goin' north! You should be out of the swamp real soon. Find a hidin' place 'til its dark."

"What 'bout you?" Lanny asked. She grabbed Joshua's arm, but he gently pried her fingers loose. "Joshua, you gotta come with us!"

"I'll catch up with you. You gotta go, Mama. Otherwise those dogs are gonna find us all standin' right here."

Lanny was shaking her head from side to side, not moving. Meaghan could hear the hounds now, baying distantly but close enough to send cold chills snaking up her spine. Those howling dogs were hunting her. Laura and Daniel looked on, eyes frightened, teeth chattering from cold and fear.

"What you gonna do?" Lanny asked.

"I'm gonna go back into the swamp and leave a trail to mix them dogs up. It'll give you time to get away," Joshua said. "You gotta go through all the streams and wet places you can find. Dogs can't get your smell from water."

Joshua placed a gentle hand on Daniel's head and kissed Lanny. "Don't you worry. I'm gonna see you real soon. Just mix up them dogs a bit, then I'll catch up. Get goin' now!"

Laura grabbed Daniel's hand and ran through the swamp. After a moment, Lanny followed, looking back once to where Joshua stood. Meaghan began to go after them, but Joshua grabbed her arm, holding her back.

"Give this to Mama for me," he said. He shoved a cold, sharp-edged object into Meaghan's hands. It was the tin box. Joshua had been carrying it the whole time.

"There's a few coins in there and two bank notes. We've had 'em a long time. Hope they's still good." He peered intently into Meaghan's face. "I don't know where you's from and you act strange, but I've a good feeling about you, girl. I know you'll help Mama and Daniel."

He reached out a hand and stroked Meaghan's hair. Meaghan stood completely still. She felt like someone had kicked her, hard, in the stomach.

A dog bayed, a high trumpeting note, almost on top of them. It rudely broke the spell that held her and Joshua.

"You best be goin'," Joshua said. He gave her his wide smile. "God willin' I'll be seein' you real soon. Take good care of yourself, Meaghan."

Meaghan jammed the tin box into her cavernous skirt pocket as she crashed headlong through the underbrush. She tripped over roots and plunged knee-deep into brackish waterholes. Thorns shredded her clothes and skin, but she didn't care. She just wanted to get away from the swamp, from the dogs, and from the pain of loss. Joshua was going from her, as Dad had done, and there was nothing she could do about it.

She easily found the others. With the dogs so close, they were concentrating on putting as much distance behind them as they could, rather than moving silently.

The swamp ended abruptly and they burst into a field of corn. Meaghan's side was aching so bad she felt split in two.

"Rest a moment," she panted.

They fell to the ground and waited for their breathing to

steady, then listened. Nothing. No dogs, no voices, just the wind whistling shrill through the high cornstalks.

"We'll be safe here awhile," Lanny said softly. "I don't want to be too far away so Joshua can't find us."

Meaghan kept her head turned from Lanny, afraid of what might be there on her face for the woman to see. Lanny gathered Daniel into her arms and lay down.

Meaghan's body ached with tiredness. She decided she would try to rest, but Laura's fingers were suddenly digging into her arm.

"You can't tell me Miss Sarah isn't a witch now," Laura hissed. "She did this to us. She put a spell on us. We're being chased by dogs, my nails are hideous, my hair will be frizzy for days from that swamp. I keep hoping it's a dream and I'll wake up at home." Her nails dug deeper into Meaghan's flesh. "She's a witch!"

Meaghan pulled her arm free, looking angrily at the red welts raised by Laura's grip.

"It's not witchcraft, it's history," she said. "And getting hysterical isn't going to help any," she added.

"Hysterical! Sure, everyone goes back in time. I'm living in history. I've been put under a spell and you say don't get hysterical!" Laura flopped back onto the dirt, staring at the sky.

She has you there. It's not witchcraft! What is it then? The black hole of time? H.G. Wells' time-travel machine?

"Do you think Lanny and Daniel make it to Canada okay?" Laura asked softly. She seemed calmer.

"Well, Miss Sarah's alive...," Meaghan thought for a moment. "...and Daniel's her grandfather, or was her grandfather..."

"It's so creepy," Laura interrupted. "We've been talking to dead people."

"They're not dead people, at least not in this time," Meaghan protested. "What was I saying? Miss Sarah's alive so Lanny and Daniel must have made it to Canada. Or," her eyes widened, "if they don't make it, Miss Sarah would never be born and someone else would be living in the cottage. Maybe we're supposed to do something. Maybe that's why we're here. Something we do makes it turn out right, or if we don't do it...would it turn out wrong?" It was like a brain teaser and she hated those.

"You mean we could change history?" Laura asked.

Meaghan shrugged. "I don't know. It's like thinking about the stars and galaxies, how they go on and on. It gets too big and confusing until even thinking about it makes my head hurt."

"But what if we don't make it to Canada? What if we're captured and we never get away?" Laura's voice was beginning to climb again. "Does that mean we won't be alive in our own time and will have to stay here forever? What if we die here? Greg would be an only child! He'd probably move into our bedroom, because it's the biggest. We wouldn't exist!" She was making fish-out-of-water gasping noises.

Meaghan stared at Laura. She was really going off her nut.

"What about our stuff?" Laura continued. "Would it just disappear from the house, fade away or something? No one would remember us. You can't remember someone who has never been."

"What?" Meaghan shook her head. She was so tired she couldn't even begin to follow Laura's frantic words. "You're going to make us crazy. I'm going to sleep."

"But what if..."

Meaghan covered her ears with her hands. Geez, she wished Laura would shut up. She hated all this talk about dying and fading away. *I never thought of death as blackness. I always believed it was light.*

Meaghan curled into a small ball and rolled onto her side away from Laura, and immediately stifled a tiny yelp. The tin box had dug into her hip. She had forgotten it was there. *All you have to do is take it out, open it, and you'd be home. It's so easy. You don't have to be here. She promised Joshua.*

Meaghan shifted, moving the box from under her. Laura was going to kill her, but for now it was staying in her skirt pocket.

○ ○ ○ ○ ○

Tiny, hot needles were pricking her ears. Meaghan sat up flapping her hands about her head in an attempt to chase the clouds of mosquitos away. She was the first one to wake and she really needed a bathroom. There were no flush toilets here so she crouched in the corn. At least it didn't stink like the ditch behind the slave cabins. She rapidly pulled her skirt down. Bare flesh was fair game for the mosquitos.

The sky was streaked purple and red as Meaghan watched the sun set in the west. In the west! It felt absurdly good to know a direction. She might not know where she was, but she knew which way was west. Laura woke up looking decidedly uncomfortable.

"The bathroom's over there," Meaghan said. She pointed into the corn. Laura grimaced but stumbled away.

Dark was falling rapidly as Meaghan woke the others. She was restless now, anxious to be on her way. They had stayed too long already. Still, Lanny held back, stretching on tip toes to see over the high corn rows.

"We've got to go, Lanny," Meaghan said.

"But what if he comes and can't find us?"

"He knows we're following the star. He'll find us." It was the awfullest lie she had ever told.

Lanny sighed, took Daniel's hand, and began to walk through a tunnel of corn.

"A person could get lost in here," Laura said nervously as she followed Lanny. She turned and glared at Meaghan. Meaghan glared back. Like this was her fault? She could feel the tin box slapping against her thigh as she walked. No doubt about it, Laura was going to kill her.

The corn ended at a dirt road. Meaghan felt exposed in the open space after the closed-in comfort of the field. Lanny stepped past her. She looked carefully up and down the road, then into the sky above her.

"It follows the star. Might be it goes all the way to Canada," Lanny said. "Be easier for Joshua to find us if we keep to a road."

Meaghan and Laura exchanged a look. Lanny had no idea of how far it was to Canada, and there was no way this road would take them all the way there.

Meaghan kept her eyes on Laura's back. She didn't want to lose sight of her. She'd never seen such blackness before, so dense she could barely see her foot in front of her. There was no moon again this night, just a faint, silver circlet in the sky to prove its existence. Her insides quivered fearfully. She must not lose the other girl—her only link to herself.

"Listen." Laura's voice was sharp and urgent, breaking into Meaghan's thoughts. She stood completely still. "I hear something coming down the road." Laura was whispering now.

Meaghan couldn't hear anything, but that didn't matter. She

could feel the danger prickling her neck and creeping down her spine. Lanny and Daniel were already running through the corn, and Meaghan and Laura quickly followed. She could hear it now—the sound of horses being ridden fast down the road.

Lanny stopped abruptly and the two girls ran into her. Through the fear that throbbed in her ears, Meaghan thought she heard the clink of metal hitting rock.

Lanny grabbed Meaghan's arm. "We gotta stop runnin'. We're makin' too much noise. Stay down!" she whispered harshly.

"I'm sure I saw somethin' run into this field." The voice was to the right. Meaghan could hear someone parting the corn, coming toward them. She tried to quiet her breathing. Lanny put her hand over Daniel's mouth. Laura was cowering in a tight ball, arms wrapped around her head.

"Probably a 'coon or rabbit." A second man was speaking, and Meaghan judged he was still on the road. "I don't think they would've come along the road. Those people are right smart at times, like foxes they are. Ain't gonna walk right down the middle of the road just waitin' for us to find 'em. I s'pect they headed right 'cross the fields and come out near the railroad tracks."

The first man grunted his agreement but continued searching the field. Meaghan was terrified. Her feet wanted to run so bad she didn't know how much longer she could stop them from going.

"Look at that fellow we caught." The second man was speaking again. "Right smart he was, leadin' the dogs in circles through the swamp so the others could get away. I'm gonna check down at the tracks. I tell you that's where they are."

"Could be you're right." The first man stopped, then turned away. After what seemed ages Meaghan heard the sound of hooves echoing down the dirt road. She lay for a long time frozen and unable to move.

Lanny was keening deeply in her throat, arms locked around her knees, rocking back and forth. Meaghan felt numb. Joshua had been taken. She had known it was going to happen, but now it was real.

"What's that?" Laura asked suddenly.

"What's what?" Meaghan could hardly speak. Her body and mind were bruised and battered. She was so incredibly scared and tired.

"Something shiny over there." Laura crawled on her hands and knees into the corn, pushing the stalks away, searching.

"This? What's this?" She sat back on her heels and stared at the shiny object in her hands—the tin money box.

"You had it all the time!" she said accusingly to Meaghan. "You had it all this time! We could have gone back. I didn't have to be here. I didn't have to be wet, cold, hungry, and scared!" she whispered fiercely, crawling closer to Meaghan.

"I don't even know if it's the box that takes us back," Meaghan said hurriedly. She began to back away from Laura. "It might not do anything."

Laura stopped. "Well, I'm going to find out," she said. "I'm going home. You can come with me or not, I don't care."

Meaghan looked helplessly at the silently sobbing Lanny. She looked at Daniel sitting motionless, all the life seemingly drained from him. *I've got a good feelin' about you girl. I know you'll help Mama and Daniel.* She didn't want to leave them, but if Laura took the box and went home without her, she'd be left here forever.

She reached over and touched the back of Lanny's hand. It was icy. "I've got to go, Lanny. I'm sorry, really sorry." The tears flowed down her face. She didn't think Lanny even heard her.

Laura worked to open the lid. Suddenly, the top flew back, and the two girls bent their heads to look into the box. Through the swirling colours, the grey, then black, Meaghan could hear Laura.

"I'll never forgive you for this. Never!"

CHAPTER 12

Meaghan walked into the kitchen, stopping in the doorway when she saw Laura at the sink eating a peach. Laura whirled around, took one look at Meaghan, and headed out the kitchen door. That suited Meaghan just fine. She was thirsty and had come to get a drink of orange juice.

She and Laura had avoided each other ever since they had found themselves back in their own time, in the middle of the lane near Miss Sarah's house. Moses had been hissing and spitting through the bars of his cage. Laura had stalked off, tin box in her hand, leaving Meaghan to stagger home, carrying the angry cat.

Meaghan drank her juice, standing at the window watching Laura swing in the hammock. To think that at one time she had actually thought Laura almost human. Obviously, time travel messed up one's perception. A memory of Laura holding Daniel's hand flashed across her mind. You just couldn't figure some people out.

"Well, what's the problem between you and Laura this time?" Her mother sounded tired. She came and stood beside Meaghan.

"Nothing," Meaghan said.

"Nothing? You two haven't spoken to each other for days. You girls...Evan and I don't know what to do."

Moses was coiling his body around Mom's legs. Boy, when he was hungry, he really went into his Dr. Jekyll act. Meaghan had yet to convince her mother that Moses had two very distinct personalities.

Meaghan shot a quick glance at her mother. She looked beat. *You're pretty selfish, you and Laura. Causing your mother all this trouble. I never thought of Mom as a person before, someone who could get tired. She was always...just Mom. You're going to have to try harder. It's Laura's fault too. You don't think they're going to divorce do you?*

That was a horrible thought. Meaghan had seen the way Evan looked at her mother and how her eyes would shine. They needed each other and Meaghan needed...well, she never thought she would admit this, but she guessed she would miss Evan and Greg if they weren't around, and would she miss...Laura?

"I'll work on it, Mom," Meaghan promised.

Her mother smiled and pulled her into her arms. "I know it's tough, honey, but thank you."

Meaghan's mother looked out the window at Laura lying in the hammock. "Now there's someone who could do with a hug, if she'd let you anywhere near her." She sighed and left the kitchen.

Meaghan remained at the window, watching how the tall, thin, afternoon shadows crept across the lawn toward Laura. Moses was on the counter, mewling and demanding attention. Meaghan ignored him. The sun had dropped behind the trees and Laura was now completely engulfed by dark. Meaghan's eyes widened with surprise. Why hadn't she seen it before? The shadows, they had given her the clue. Laura, too, was a prey of the blackness.

An unsheathed claw shot out, leaving a painful red trail down Meaghan's arm.

"You dumb cat!" she yelled. She opened the pantry and got out a can of cat food. She looked at the label. It was different from the brand Miss Sarah had given them. In fact, now that she thought about it, hadn't Mom said something about having to buy more cat food? But Miss Sarah had said she would be back in three days time, by Friday. It was now Wednesday of the following week. She had been gone eight days. Meaghan spooned the food into Moses' bowl. Eight days!

○ ○ ○ ○ ○

Meaghan slammed the book shut with a bang. She had read the whole thing from cover to cover and there was nothing, not one reference or a single clue, to tell her that Lanny and Daniel had made it safely to Canada. She tossed the book on to her night table and turned out the light. It had been a long shot at best. Thousands of slaves had escaped and the book had interviewed only a handful of them. Still, she had really thought there might be something in all that small print.

She slid further down in the bed and pulled the cotton sheet over her. It was really too hot to cover up, but for some reason she felt better with the sheet secure about her neck. Probably because of the dreams.

She listened to Laura's regular breathing. She felt like throwing a pillow at her. It was indecent the way Laura slept so soundly. Meaghan yanked her pillow from under her head, sighed, fluffed it, and slipped it back in place.

It was a miracle she wasn't a total basketcase. First she couldn't get to sleep at all because of the dark, then just as she was getting used to that and could sleep—wanted to sleep—she was scared to close her eyes. Sleep meant dreams, strange dreams that disturbed and beckoned and, upon waking, left her stomach knotted with dread.

Meaghan heard Moses patter into the room. She tensed then relaxed as the cat jumped on to Laura's bed. Eight days. Miss Sarah would never leave her garden for eight days.

Purple and black storm clouds massed on the horizon, yet the sky under which Meaghan stood was deep blue. She was in a small clearing, trees encircling her on three sides, the fourth open. A cold wind showered her with swirls of red, yellow, and orange. Meaghan shivered and hugged her tattered blouse to her body. A path rose steeply in front of her. Meaghan began to follow it, rounded a large boulder and saw a cave before her. Sheer stone walls rose above her on each side. There was no way around, no where to go except on the path, and it led directly into the cave.

The light was fading rapidly. Meaghan looked up and saw the storm clouds were boiling and churning above her, blotting out the sun. Lightning, white and forked, stabbed the ground behind her. The blast was deafening, but over it Meaghan could hear the sound of a hoe scratching from inside the cave. Miss Sarah...or a trick of the blackness?

The storm burst furiously on Meaghan; rain blinded her and the wind tore at her skirt. She had to find shelter. Someone was calling her name and Meaghan climbed further up the path. The rain eased a moment and she saw her father, standing in the dark mouth of the cave, calling and waving to her to come; come with him into the blackness. She didn't want to go, but Dad was calling her name, again and again. Finally he turned and went into the cave alone. Meaghan screamed at him not to go.

"Meaghan! Meaghan! Wake up!" Laura had her by the shoulders and was shaking her.

"I'm awake, I'm awake," Meaghan said. She was getting whiplash. She struggled to sit up. Her T-shirt was soaked with sweat, yet her teeth chattered.

"You scared me half to death yelling like that," Laura grumbled. She bounced on the side of Meaghan's bed. "Do you want a drink or something? Your mom?"

The idea of Mom fussing over her was tempting, but Meaghan shook her head. "No, let her sleep. Though I'm surprised she's not here already. When I was little and had bad dreams, she always came before I even called her."

"I guess she would. You scream like a banshee. You almost gave me a heart attack," Laura said. "You don't have these nightmares often, do you? I really need my sleep."

That was Laura for you. Always concerned for the other guy. But she had woken Meaghan up.

"When I was little," Laura was saying, "my mom would come in too. Put on the light, tell me everything was okay and tuck me in." She gave a bitter half-laugh. "Could care less about me now."

Meaghan saw Laura alone in the hammock, the shadows creeping over her.

"I don't think that's true," Meaghan said. Laura snorted. "I think it's like Miss Sarah said, your mom's off track right now. You know, I bet it hasn't anything to do with you at all. It's just her. It's her problem."

"You know, I go there and I see her and her new husband and a new baby, and it's like I don't exist for her any more. Then Dad married your mother, you moved in, and everything's so different. I don't fit in anywhere; there's no place for me. No one wants me." Laura walked over to Meaghan's dresser, opened a drawer and pulled out a T-shirt.

"You better put this on, your other one's drenched." She threw it to Meaghan, crossed to the window, and looked out. "No one can sleep in this heat."

Remembering Laura's steady breathing, Meaghan grinned.

"I'm going to tell Dad he has to get us an air conditioner for this room," Laura went on. "I'll tell him the heat's giving you nightmares."

Meaghan stripped off her T-shirt, tossed it on the floor, and pulled on the clean one.

"Thanks, Laura," she said.

"Yeah, all right." Laura flopped onto her own bed.

"No really, I'm glad you woke me. If you're ever having a bad dream, I'll do the same for you," Meaghan said. Why wasn't Mom ever around to hear the good stuff? But Mom was around, watching her, watching Laura in the hammock.

"Laura," she said. "Any time you want, my mom would come and tuck you in. Just give her a chance."

"Oh, geez," Laura said loudly. "This stupid cat. Just what I need, a fur rug for my feet in 100 degree heat."

Meaghan sat up in bed, the urgency of her dream returning. "Moses. Laura, Mom had to buy more cat food."

"So what."

"We used up all the food Miss Sarah gave us. Don't you see? She didn't plan to be away this long. Something's wrong, really wrong." Meaghan got out of bed and stood over Laura. "You asked me what would happen if Lanny and Daniel didn't make it to Canada. Would Miss Sarah be alive? She's been gone so long, I'm beginning to think they didn't make it. Laura, we've got to go back. Something's wrong. I don't think Miss Sarah is ever coming home."

Laura propped a pillow behind her back. "I'm not going back. Ever. There's nothing we can do. We can't change anything."

"I've got to try. I'll go back by myself if I have to. Where's the box?"

"I threw it away," Laura said.

"You what!"

"Don't get all excited. I didn't really throw it away. Just giving you back some of your own, if you know what I mean."

Laura walked over to her bookcase, pulled a few books out, and reached into the emptied space. She brought out the box and sat it on Meaghan's bed.

"I'm impressed," she said. "You don't snoop. You could have found it in a minute if you'd looked."

"I like my privacy. I just take it for granted you like yours," Meaghan said absently. She was running her fingers over a dent in the side of the box. She remembered the *clink* in the cornfield before Laura found the box. It brought back other memories of being scared, tired, dirty, cold, and hungry. *Are you really going back? Why? She promised Joshua. It's so awful there and what if this time you don't get home. Lanny and Daniel are willing to go through anything to be free. She's got to go back. I liked you better when you were a wimp.*

"Are you really going to do it?" Laura asked.

"Yeah. Yeah, I am. And it's all because of you."

"Because of me?"

"This all began that day when you and those kids went by in the red pickup. That started it and I'm going to finish it," Meaghan said. She went to her own bookcase, pulled out a couple of books, reached behind, and brought out a square wooden box. "But this time, I'm taking some stuff with me."

She dumped the contents of the wooden box onto her bed and began selecting different items. "Compass, my dad's old pocket knife, see it's got a fork and spoon, matches..." She got up and ran to the bathroom, returning shortly. "...toothbrush and paste. I hate not brushing my teeth."

"Do you think this stuff will go back with you?" Laura asked.

"I hope so. I figured I'd put it in the tin."

Meaghan dropped everything into the tin box, being careful not to look inside it.

"Guess that's everything," she said. She looked around the room. "I better go now, before I lose my nerve."

Meaghan placed the tin on her knee and bent her head over the box.

"Wait! I'm going with you!" Through the swirling colours, then the grey, Meaghan saw Laura tumble off the bed and stretch out a hand toward her. "Wait for me!"

CHAPTER 13

She was in her dream! Meaghan stood in an open space in the woods, on a slight rise that allowed her a clear view in front of her. Purple storm clouds loomed on the horizon, and a gusty wind blew coloured leaves in tiny, whirling tornados about her feet. A hard-packed dirt path climbed steeply beside her, winding past a large, jutting rock and out of view. The tin box had taken her into her dream! Dream? This was a nightmare!

"Where're Lanny and Daniel?"

Meaghan spun around. Laura was standing behind her, looking puzzled. Meaghan took the skin of Laura's upper arm between her thumb and index finger and pinched hard.

"What did you do that for?" Laura cried.

Laura was real.

Meaghan turned back and studied the clouds. They were different from the ones in her dream, but she couldn't figure out why. Then she knew—they weren't moving! In her dream the clouds had been drawing closer and closer to her, but these were piled one on top of the other, motionless.

"They're mountains, Laura. We're in the mountains! I thought they were clouds. I thought I was in my dream."

The land stretched away from them in coloured ripples. The slopes closest to them were dark green and blue, densely covered with evergreens; those farther away, a dark, fuzzy mauve.

"Shouldn't Lanny and Daniel be here?" Laura asked again.

"They must be nearby. Every other time they've been here," Meaghan answered. "We'll have to look around."

She spilled the contents of the tin box on the ground, then held up the compass.

"Everything came through all right," she said. She swung the compass about in a circle, watching its gyrating needle. "That's north, so we better go that way." Her voice faltered. Going north meant going up the path. She might not be in her dream, but the resemblance was so close it was scary.

"Where do you think we are?" Laura asked.

Meaghan thought for a moment. She had been doing a lot of reading about the Underground Railroad and escaped slaves and had studied maps of South Carolina, trying to figure out where they had been. She had even found an old National Geographic map that showed the various routes runaways took.

"I think we're in the mountains in North Carolina," she said. "There're mountains that start in the north part of South Carolina, go into North Carolina and then into Virginia."

She shuffled her feet though yellowed leaves.

"Dead leaves," Laura said. "It must be fall." She looked up at the trees. "I'd say late October. The branches are pretty bare." She pointed at a trail through the trees. "There's a path going that way. I wonder if animals made it, big animals."

"I read that Indians travelled in these mountains a lot and runaway slaves followed their trails all the time," Meaghan said.

"Well, I wish those books you always have your nose in told you where Daniel and Lanny are," said Laura. "Let's go. Watch those roots sticking out."

Laura started up the path, Meaghan following close behind.

Gloom was gathering and the lower slopes of the mountains were darkening with approaching night.

"Lanny! Daniel!" Laura shouted.

Meaghan grabbed the other girl's shoulder and swung her around.

"What are you doing? Letting everyone know we're here? What if there're slavecatchers out there?"

"Oh, yeah, I didn't think about that."

Laura continued leading the way, moving slower now; it was becoming difficult to see the trail. She stopped abruptly and stood completely still.

"What? What?"

"Shhh...." Laura held up her hand to quiet Meaghan. She was listening intently. All Meaghan could hear was a trickle of water nearby, the soft murmur of the trees, and a thud and snuffling sound in the woods to the right of her that made her step closer to Laura.

"What do you hear?" She whispered.

"I don't know." Laura's voice was low. "It's coming from over there." She pointed to the right of the path. Great, right where the snuffling sound was. "We better check it out."

Laura left the trail, pushing branches and brush from her way. Meaghan followed, holding Laura's skirt with one hand and her father's army knife in the other. She flipped one of the blades open. *Great protection against a bear. You cut a teeny bit out of him and he takes a big chunk out of you.* She glanced down at her hand and saw she had flipped up the spoon. *Fighting wildlife with an eating utensil?*

The trees opened up suddenly, and they almost banged their noses against a stone wall. It was growing difficult to see

114

Laura, a doctor! She never opened a book. There's a lot more to this girl than blue eyes and red lips. You been looking at her, but not seeing.

"If only I could do something for Lanny," Laura was saying.

"She's still alive," Meaghan pointed out. "You know, I've been looking at the North Star all night, and I have this feeling that everything's going to be okay."

"A feeling? You sound like Miss Sarah. Practicing witchcraft?"

"I'd practice anything right about now, if it would help Lanny." Meaghan tossed a piece of wood into the fire and watched white sparks rise into the clear morning air. "I'm going to get some more water."

Meaghan waded into the stream, cupped water in her hands and splashed it on her face, then drank. Mom would have fits if she knew they were drinking straight out of a stream. She was dipping the tin box into the water, when she heard the sound of an axe cutting into wood.

With the half-filled box in her hand, Meaghan crossed the stream and scrambled up the opposite bank. Her feet slid out from under her on the dew-wet grass, but she managed to grab a vine to stop her fall. The box tumbled from her hand into the stream, clanging on rocks as it fell. Meaghan hastily skidded down the side and fished the box from the stream. There was no way she was leaving it behind this time. She pushed it deep into her pocket and climbed back up. She hid behind a wide tree trunk and peered out.

A wooden house stood in the middle of a field of stumps, a curl of smoke rising white from its chimney. The chopping sounds were coming from behind it. Then suddenly they stopped. Meaghan wondered if there was any chance she could sneak into the house and find some food. She leaned out further to look at the house again.

A hand came down hard, gripping her shoulder and yanking her to her feet. She screamed and struggled.

"Hush girl. I'm not going to hurt thee," a deep voice growled at her. Meaghan looked up terrified. It was a white man, as big as a bear; he had a bear's huge, shaggy head, thick black eyebrows, and large white teeth. The hand holding her dropped away, and Meaghan saw the palm and fingers were as large as a shovel.

"Didn't mean to scare thee, just wondered who was sneaking around my property," the man said. It was like listening to gravel roll around in a cement mixer. "That your fire up on the ridge?" He gestured with the axe he held in the direction Meaghan had come. Meaghan nodded.

The man looked at her thoughtfully. "Thee all alone, girl?"

"Yes," she said.

"Are thee a runaway slave?"

Meaghan felt her chest tighten. She wanted to shake her head, deny it, run far from him, but this was the only opportunity she had to get food. Something was niggling at the corner of her mind, something about his clothes—grey, plain, unadorned—his peculiar manner of speaking, something she had read...

Quakers! Quakers dressed plainly, and spoke funny, and, most importantly, they also helped runaway slaves. Was this man a Quaker? Meaghan looked again into the man's grey eyes, seeing what she had, in her fear, missed before—kindness and caring. She took a deep breath.

"In a cave on the ridge are two escaped slaves, a mother and

120

ABOUT THE AUTHOR

Barbara Haworth-Attard lives in London, Ontario, with her husband and two school-aged sons. Before entering the fiction field, she wrote scripts for a Canadian educational media company. This is her first junior novel.

ACKNOWLEDGEMENTS

Thank you to the Writers' Group – Maggie, Kim, and Norah – who help make the words flow. A special thank you to Joe.

PRINTED BY
IMPRIMERIE D'ÉDITION MARQUIS
IN MAY 1995
MONTMAGNY (QUÉBEC)